Joseph Lewis French

Riddle Stories

Joseph Lewis French

Riddle Stories

ISBN/EAN: 9783955630379

Auflage: 1

Erscheinungsjahr: 2013

Erscheinungsort: Bremen, Deutschland

@ Leseklassiker in Access Verlag GmbH, Fahrenheitstr. 1, 28359 Bremen. Alle Rechte beim Verlag und bei den jeweiligen Lizenzgebern.

Leseklassiker

Foreword

A distinguished American writer of fiction said to me lately: "Did you ever think of the vital American way we live? We are always going after mental gymnastics." Now the mystery story is mental gymnastics. By the time the reader has followed a chain of facts through he has exercised his mind, — given himself a mental breather. But the claims of the true mystery story do not end with the general reader. It is entitled to the consideration of the discriminating because it indubitably takes its own place as a gauge of mastery in the field of the short story.

The demand was never quite so keen as it is now. The currents of literature as of all things change swiftly these times. This world of ours has become very sophisticated. It has suffered itself to be exploited till there is no external wonder left. Retroactively the demand for mystery, which is the very soul of interest, must find new expression. Thus we turn inward for fresh thrills to the human comedy, and outward to the realm of the supernatural.

The riddle story is the most naïve form of the mystery story. It may contain a certain element of the supernatural — be tinged with mysticism — but its motive and the revelation thereof must be frankly materialistic — of the earth, earthy. In this respect it is very closely allied to the detective story. The model riddle story should be utterly mundane in motive — told in direct terms. Here again the genius of that great modern master asserts itself, and in "The Oblong Box" we have an early model of its kind. The stories of this collection cover a wide range and are the choice of reading in several literatures.

Joseph Lewis French.

Contents

I. The Mysterious Card — Cleveland Moffett	1
II. The Great Valdez Sapphir — (Anonymous)	37
III. The Oblong Box — Edgar Allan Poe	64
IV. The Birth-Mark — Nathaniel Hawthorne	80
V. A Terribly Strange Bed — Wilkie Collins	104
VI. The Torture by Hope — Villiers de l'Isle Adam	127
VII. The Box with the Iron Clamps — Florence Marryat	134
VIII. My Fascinating Friend — William Archer	178
IX. The Lost Room — Fitz-James O'Brien	199

I. The Mysterious Card — Cleveland Moffett

I

Richard Burwell, of New York, will never cease to regret that the French language was not made a part of his education.

This is why:

On the second evening after Burwell arrived in Paris, feeling lonely without his wife and daughter, who were still visiting a friend in London, his mind naturally turned to the theatre. So, after consulting the daily amusement calendar, he decided to visit the Folies Bergère, which he had heard of as one of the notable sights. During an intermission he went into the beautiful garden, where gay crowds were strolling among the flowers, and lights, and fountains. He had just seated himself at a little three-legged table, with a view to enjoying the novel scene, when his attention was attracted by a lovely woman, gowned strikingly, though in perfect taste, who passed near him, leaning on the arm of a gentleman. The only thing that he noticed about this gentleman was that he wore eye-glasses.

Now Burwell had never posed as a captivator of the fair sex, and could scarcely credit his eyes when the lady left the side of her escort and, turning back as if she had forgotten something, passed close by him, and deftly placed a card on his table. The card bore some French words written in purple ink, but, not knowing that language, he was unable to make out their meaning. The lady paid no further heed to him, but, rejoining the gentleman with the eye-glasses, swept out of the place with the grace and dignity of a princess. Burwell remained staring at the card.

Needless to say, he thought no more of the performance or of the other attractions about him. Everything seemed flat and tawdry compared with the radiant vision that had appeared and disappeared so mysteriously. His one desire now was to discover the meaning of the words written on the card.

Calling a fiácre, he drove to the Hôtel Continental, where he was staying. Proceeding directly to the office and taking the manager aside, Burwell asked if he would be kind enough to translate a few words of French into English. There were no more than twenty words in all.

"Why, certainly," said the manager, with French politeness, and cast his eyes over the card. As he read, his face grew rigid with astonishment, and, looking at his questioner sharply, he exclaimed: "Where did you get this, monsieur?"

Burwell started to explain, but was interrupted by: "That will do, that will do. You must leave the hotel."

"What do you mean?" asked the man from New York, in amazement.

"You must leave the hotel now — to-night — without fail," commanded the manager excitedly.

Now it was Burwell's turn to grow angry, and he declared heatedly that if he wasn't wanted in this hotel there were plenty of others in Paris where he would be welcome. And, with an assumption of dignity, but piqued at heart, he settled his bill, sent for his belongings, and drove up the Rue de la Paix to the Hôtel Bellevue, where he spent the night.

The next morning he met the proprietor, who seemed to be a good fellow, and, being inclined now to view the incident of the previous evening from its ridiculous side, Burwell explained what had befallen him, and was pleased to find a sympathetic listener.

"Why, the man was a fool," declared the proprietor. "Let me see the card; I will tell you what it means." But as he read, his face and manner changed instantly.

"This is a serious matter," he said sternly. "Now I understand why my confrère refused to entertain you. I regret, monsieur, but I shall be obliged to do as he did."

"What do you mean?"

"Simply that you cannot remain here."

With that he turned on his heel, and the indignant guest could not prevail upon him to give any explanation.

"We'll see about this," said Burwell, thoroughly angered.

It was now nearly noon, and the New Yorker remembered an engagement to lunch with a friend from Boston, who, with his family, was stopping at the Hôtel de l'Alma. With his luggage on the carriage, he ordered the *cocher* to drive directly there, determined to take counsel with his countryman before selecting new quarters. His friend was highly indignant when he heard the story — a fact that gave Burwell no little comfort, knowing, as he did, that the man was accustomed to foreign ways from long residence abroad.

"It is some silly mistake, my dear fellow; I wouldn't pay any attention to it. Just have your luggage taken down and stay here. It is a nice, homelike place, and it will be very jolly, all being together. But, first, let me prepare a little 'nerve settler' for you."

After the two had lingered a moment over their Manhattan cocktails, Burwell's friend excused himself to call the ladies. He had proceeded only two or three steps when he turned, and said: "Let's see that mysterious card that has raised all this row."

He had scarcely withdrawn it from Burwell's hand when he started back, and exclaimed: —

"Great God, man! Do you mean to say — this is simply — "

Then, with a sudden movement of his hand to his head, he left the room.

He was gone perhaps five minutes, and when he returned his face was white.

"I am awfully sorry," he said nervously; "but the ladies tell me they — that is, my wife — she has a frightful headache. You will have to excuse us from the lunch."

Instantly realizing that this was only a flimsy pretense, and deeply hurt by his friend's behaviour, the mystified man arose at once and left without another word. He was now determined to solve this mystery at any cost. What could be the meaning of the words on that infernal piece of pasteboard?

Profiting by his humiliating experiences, he took good care not to show the card to any one at the hotel where he now established himself, — a comfortable little place near the Grand Opera House.

All through the afternoon he thought of nothing but the card, and turned over in his mind various ways of learning its meaning without getting himself into further trouble. That evening he went again to the *Folies Bergère* in the hope of finding the mysterious woman, for he was now more than ever anxious to discover who she was. It even occurred to him that she might be one of those beautiful Nihilist conspirators, or, perhaps, a Russian spy, such as he had read of in novels. But he failed to find her, either then or on the three subsequent evenings which he passed in the same place. Meanwhile the card was burning in his pocket like a hot coal. He dreaded the thought of meeting anyone that he knew, while this horrible cloud hung over him. He bought a French-English dictionary and tried to pick out the meaning word by word, but failed. It was all Greek to him. For the first time in his life, Burwell regretted that he had not studied French at college.

After various vain attempts to either solve or forget the torturing riddle, he saw no other course than to lay the problem before a detective agency. He accordingly put his case in the hands of an *agent de la sûreté* who was recommended as a competent and trustworthy man. They had a talk together in a private room, and, of course, Burwell showed the card. To his relief, his adviser at least showed no sign of taking offence. Only he did not and would not explain what the words meant.

"It is better," he said, "that monsieur should not know the nature of this document for the present. I will do myself the honour to call upon monsieur tomorrow at his hotel, and then monsieur shall know everything."

"Then it is really serious?" asked the unfortunate man.

"Very serious," was the answer.

The next twenty-four hours Burwell passed in a fever of anxiety. As his mind conjured up one fearful possibility after another he deeply regretted that he had not torn up the miserable card at the start. He even seized it, — prepared to strip it into fragments, and so end the whole affair. And then his Yankee stubbornness again asserted itself, and he determined to see the thing out, come what might.

"After all," he reasoned, "it is no crime for a man to pick up a card that a lady drops on his table."

Crime or no crime, however, it looked very much as if he had committed some grave offence when, the next day, his detective drove up in a carriage, accompanied by a uniformed official, and requested the astounded American to accompany them to the police headquarters.

"What for?" he asked.

"It is only a formality," said the detective; and when Burwell still protested the man in uniform remarked: "You'd better come quietly, monsieur; you will have to come, anyway."

An hour later, after severe cross-examination by another official, who demanded many facts about the New Yorker's age, place of birth, residence, occupation, etc., the bewildered man found himself in the Conciergerie prison. Why he was there or what was about to befall him Burwell had no means of knowing; but before the day was over he succeeded in having a message sent to the American Legation, where he demanded immediate protection as a citizen of the United States. It was not until evening, however, that the Secretary of

Legation, a consequential person, called at the prison. There followed a stormy interview, in which the prisoner used some strong language, the French officers gesticulated violently and talked very fast, and the Secretary calmly listened to both sides, said little, and smoked a good cigar.

"I will lay your case before the American minister," he said as he rose to go, "and let you know the result to-morrow."

"But this is an outrage. Do you mean to say — " Before he could finish, however, the Secretary, with a strangely suspicious glance, turned and left the room.

That night Burwell slept in a cell.

The next morning he received another visit from the non-committal Secretary, who informed him that matters had been arranged, and that he would be set at liberty forthwith.

"I must tell you, though," he said, "that I have had great difficulty in accomplishing this, and your liberty is granted only on condition that you leave the country within twenty-four hours, and never under any conditions return."

Burwell stormed, raged, and pleaded; but it availed nothing. The Secretary was inexorable, and yet he positively refused to throw any light upon the causes of this monstrous injustice.

"Here is your card," he said, handing him a large envelope closed with the seal of Legation. "I advise you to burn it and never refer to the matter again."

That night the ill-fated man took the train for London, his heart consumed by hatred for the whole French nation, together with a burning desire for vengeance. He wired his wife to meet him at the station, and for a long time debated with himself whether he should at once tell her the sickening truth. In the end he decided that it was better to keep silent. No sooner, however, had she seen him than her woman's instinct told her that he was labouring under some mental strain. And he saw in a moment that to withhold from her his burning secret was impossible, especially when she began to talk of the trip they had planned through France. Of course no trivial reason would satisfy her for his refusal to make this trip, since they had been looking forward to it for years; and yet it was impossible now for him to set foot on French soil.

So he finally told her the whole story, she laughing and weeping in turn. To her, as to him, it seemed incredible that such overwhelming disasters could have grown out of so small a cause, and, being a fluent French scholar, she demanded a sight of the fatal piece of pasteboard. In vain her husband tried to divert her by proposing a trip through Italy. She would consent to nothing until she had seen the mysterious card which Burwell was now convinced he ought long ago to have destroyed. After refusing for awhile to let her see it, he finally yielded. But, although he had learned to dread the consequences of showing that cursed card, he was little prepared for what followed. She read it turned pale, gasped for breath, and nearly fell to the floor.

"I told you not to read it," he said; and then, growing tender at the sight of her distress, he took her hand in his and begged her to be calm. "At least tell me what the thing means," he said. "We can bear it together; you surely can trust me."

But she, as if stung by rage, pushed him from her and declared, in a tone such as he had never heard from her before, that never, never again would she live with him. "You are a monster!" she exclaimed. And those were the last words he heard from her lips.

Failing utterly in all efforts at reconciliation, the half-crazed man took the first steamer for New York, having suffered in scarcely a fortnight more than in all his previous life. His whole pleasure trip had been ruined, he had failed to consummate important business arrangements, and now he saw his home broken up and his happiness ruined. During the voyage he scarcely left his stateroom, but lay there prostrated with agony. In this black despondency the one thing that sustained him was the thought of meeting his partner, Jack Evelyth, the friend of his boyhood, the sharer of his success, the bravest, most loyal fellow in the world. In the face of even the most damning circumstances, he felt that Evelyth's rugged common sense would evolve some way of escape from this hideous nightmare. Upon landing at New York he hardly waited for the gang-plank to be lowered before he rushed on shore and grasped the hand of his partner, who was waiting on the wharf.

"Jack," was his first word, "I am in dreadful trouble, and you are the only man in the world who can help me."

An hour later Burwell sat at his friend's dinner table, talking over the situation.

Evelyth was all kindness, and several times as he listened to Burwell's story his eyes filled with tears.

"It does not seem possible, Richard," he said, "that such things can be; but I will stand by you; we will fight it out together. But we cannot strike in the dark. Let me see this card."

"There is the damned thing," Burwell said, throwing it on the table.

Evelyth opened the envelope, took out the card, and fixed his eyes on the sprawling purple characters.

"Can you read it?" Burwell asked excitedly.

"Perfectly," his partner said. The next moment he turned pale, and his voice broke. Then he clasped the tortured man's hand in his with a strong grip. "Richard," he said slowly, "if my only child had been brought here dead it would not have caused me more sorrow than this does. You have brought me the worst news one man could bring another."

His agitation and genuine suffering affected Burwell like a death sentence.

"Speak, man," he cried; "do not spare me. I can bear anything rather than this awful uncertainty. Tell me what the card means."

Evelyth took a swallow of brandy and sat with head bent on his clasped hands.

"No, I can't do it; there are some things a man must not do."

Then he was silent again, his brows knitted. Finally he said solemnly: —

"No, I can't see any other way out of it. We have been true to each other all our lives; we have worked together and looked forward to never separating. I would rather fail and die than see this happen. But we have got to separate, old friend; we have got to separate."

They sat there talking until late into the night. But nothing that Burwell could do or say availed against his friend's decision. There was nothing for it but that Evelyth should buy his partner's share of the business or that Burwell buy out the other. The man was more than fair in the financial proposition he made; he was generous, as he always had been, but his determination was inflexible; the two must separate. And they did.

With his old partner's desertion, it seemed to Burwell that the world was leagued against him. It was only three weeks from the day on which he had received the mysterious card; yet in that time he had lost all that he valued in the world, — wife, friends, and business. What next to do with the fatal card was the sickening problem that now possessed him.

He dared not show it; yet he dared not destroy it. He loathed it; yet he could not let it go from his possession. Upon returning to his house he locked the accursed thing away in his safe as if it had been a package of dynamite or a bottle of deadly poison. Yet not a day passed that he did not open the drawer where the thing was kept and scan with loathing the mysterious purple scrawl.

In desperation he finally made up his mind to take up the study of the language in which the hateful thing was written. And still he dreaded the approach of the day when he should decipher its awful meaning.

One afternoon, less than a week after his arrival in New York, as he was crossing Twenty-third Street on the way to his French teacher, he saw a carriage rolling up Broadway. In the carriage was a face that caught his attention like a flash. As he looked again he recognized the woman who had been the cause of his undoing. Instantly he sprang into another cab and ordered the driver to follow after. He found the house where she was living. He called there several times; but always received the same reply, that she was too much engaged to see anyone. Next he was told that she was ill, and on the following day the servant said she was much worse. Three physicians had been summoned in consultation. He sought out one of these and told him it was a matter of life or death that he see this woman. The doctor was a kindly man and promised to assist him. Through his influence, it came about that on that very night Burwell stood by the bedside of this mysterious woman. She was beautiful still, though her face was worn with illness.

"Do you recognize me?" he asked tremblingly, as he leaned over the bed, clutching in one hand an envelope containing the mysterious card. "Do you remember seeing me at the *Folies Bergère* a month ago?"

"Yes," she murmured, after a moment's study of his face; and he noted with relief that she spoke English.

"Then, for God's sake, tell me, what does it all mean?" he gasped, quivering with excitement.

"I gave you the card because I wanted you to — to — "

Here a terrible spasm of coughing shook her whole body, and she fell back exhausted.

An agonizing despair tugged at Burwell's heart. Frantically snatching the card from its envelope, he held it close to the woman's face.

"Tell me! Tell me!"

With a supreme effort, the pale figure slowly raised itself on the pillow, its fingers clutching at the counterpane.

Then the sunken eyes fluttered — forced themselves open — and stared in stony amazement upon the fatal card, while the trembling lips moved noiselessly, as if in an attempt to speak. As Burwell, choking with eagerness, bent his head slowly to hers, a suggestion of a smile flickered across the woman's face. Again the mouth quivered, the man's head bent nearer and nearer to hers, his eyes riveted upon the lips. Then, as if to aid her in deciphering the mystery, he turned his eyes to the card.

With a cry of horror he sprang to his feet, his eyeballs starting from their sockets. Almost at the same moment the woman fell heavily upon the pillow.

Every vestige of the writing had faded! The card was blank!

The woman lay there dead.

II

The Card Unveiled

No physician was ever more scrupulous than I have been, during my thirty years of practice, in observing the code of professional secrecy; and it is only for grave reasons, partly in the interests of medical science, largely as a warning to intelligent people, that I place upon record the following statements.

One morning a gentleman called at my offices to consult me about some nervous trouble. From the moment I saw him, the man made a deep impression on me, not so much by the pallor and worn look of his face as by a certain intense sadness in his eyes, as if all hope had gone out of his life. I wrote a prescription for him, and advised him to try the benefits of an ocean voyage. He seemed to shiver at the idea, and said that he had been abroad too much, already.

As he handed me my fee, my eye fell upon the palm of his hand, and I saw there, plainly marked on the Mount of Saturn, a cross surrounded by two circles. I should explain that for the greater part of my life I have been a constant and enthusiastic student of palmistry. During my travels in the Orient, after taking my degree, I spent months studying this fascinating art at the best sources of information in the world. I have read everything published on palmistry in every known language, and my library on the subject is perhaps the most complete in existence. In my time I have examined at least fourteen thousand palms, and taken casts of many of the more interesting of them. But I had never seen such a palm as this; at least, never but once, and the horror of the case was so great that I shudder even now when I call it to mind.

"Pardon me," I said, keeping the patient's hand in mine, "would you let me look at your palm?"

I tried to speak indifferently, as if the matter were of small consequence, and for some moments I bent over the hand in silence. Then, taking a magnifying glass from my desk, I looked at it still more closely. I was not mistaken; here was indeed the sinister double circle on Saturn's mount, with the cross inside, — a marking so rare as to portend some stupendous destiny of good or evil, more probably the latter.

I saw that the man was uneasy under my scrutiny, and, presently, with some hesitation, as if mustering courage, he asked: "Is there anything remarkable about my hand?"

"Yes," I said, "there is. Tell me, did not something very unusual, something very horrible, happen to you about ten or eleven years ago?"

I saw by the way the man started that I had struck near the mark, and, studying the stream of fine lines that crossed his lifeline from the Mount of Venus, I added: "Were you not in some foreign country at that time?"

The man's face blanched, but he only looked at me steadily out of those mournful eyes. Now I took his other hand, and compared the two, line by line, mount by mount, noting the short square fingers, the heavy thumb, with amazing willpower in its upper joint, and gazing again and again at that ominous sign on Saturn.

"Your life has been strangely unhappy, your years have been clouded by some evil influence."

"My God," he said weakly, sinking into a chair, "how can you know these things?"

"It is easy to know what one sees," I said, and tried to draw him out about his past, but the words seemed to stick in his throat.

"I will come back and talk to you again," he said, and he went away without giving me his name or any revelation of his life.

Several times he called during subsequent weeks, and gradually seemed to take on a measure of confidence in my presence. He would talk freely of his physical condition, which seemed to cause him much anxiety. He even insisted upon my making the most careful examination of all his organs, especially of his eyes, which, he said, had troubled him at various times. Upon making the usual tests, I found that he was suffering from a most uncommon form of colour blindness, that seemed to vary in its manifestations, and to be connected with certain hallucinations or abnormal mental states which recurred periodically, and about which I had great difficulty in persuading him to speak. At each visit I took occasion to study his hand anew, and each reading of the palm gave me stronger conviction that here was a life mystery that would abundantly repay any pains taken in unravelling it.

While I was in this state of mind, consumed with a desire to know more of my unhappy acquaintance and yet not daring to press him with questions, there came a tragic happening that revealed to me with startling suddenness the secret I was bent on knowing. One night, very late, — in fact it was about four o'clock in the morning, — I received an urgent summons to the bedside of a man who had been shot. As I bent over him I saw that it was my friend, and for the first time I realized that he was a man of wealth and position, for he lived in a beautifully furnished house filled with art treasures and looked after by a retinue of servants. From one of these I learned that he was Richard Burwell, one of New York's most respected citizens — in fact, one of her best-known philanthropists, a man who for years had devoted his life and fortune to good works among the poor.

But what most excited my surprise was the presence in the house of two officers, who informed me that Mr. Burwell was under arrest, charged with murder. The officers assured me that it was only out of deference to his well-known standing in the community that the prisoner had been allowed the privilege of receiving medical treatment in his own home; their orders were peremptory to keep him under close surveillance.

Giving no time to further questionings, I at once proceeded to examine the injured man, and found that he was suffering from a bullet wound in the back at about the height of the fifth rib. On probing for the bullet, I found that it had lodged near the heart, and decided that it would be exceedingly dangerous to try to remove it immediately. So I contented myself with administering a sleeping potion.

As soon as I was free to leave Burwell's bedside I returned to the officers and obtained from them details of what had happened. A woman's body had been found a few hours before, shockingly mutilated, on Water Street, one of the dark ways in the swarming region along the river front. It had been found at about two o'clock in the morning by some printers from the office of the *Courier des Etats Unis*, who, in coming from their work, had heard cries of distress and hurried to the rescue. As they drew near they saw a man spring away from something huddled on the sidewalk, and plunge into the shadows of the night, running from them at full speed.

Suspecting at once that here was the mysterious assassin so long vainly sought for many similar crimes, they dashed after the fleeing man, who darted right and left through the maze of dark streets, giving out little cries like a squirrel as he ran.

Seeing that they were losing ground, one of the printers fired at the fleeing shadow, his shot being followed by a scream of pain, and hurrying up they found a man writhing on the ground. The man was Richard Burwell.

The news that my sad-faced friend had been implicated in such a revolting occurrence shocked me inexpressibly, and I was greatly relieved the next day to learn from the papers that a most unfortunate mistake had been made. The evidence given before the coroner's jury was such as to abundantly exonerate Burwell from all shadow of guilt. The man's own testimony, taken at his bedside, was in itself almost conclusive in his favour. When asked to explain his presence so late at night in such a part of the city, Burwell stated that he had spent the evening at the Florence Mission, where he had made an address to some unfortunates gathered there, and that later he had gone with a young missionary worker to visit a woman living on Frankfort Street, who was dying of consumption. This statement was borne out by the missionary worker himself, who testified that Burwell had been most tender in his ministrations to the poor woman and had not left her until death had relieved her sufferings.

Another point which made it plain that the printers had mistaken their man in the darkness, was the statement made by all of them that, as they came running up, they had overheard some words spoken by the murderer, and that these words were in their own language, French. Now it was shown conclusively that Burwell did not know the French language, that indeed he had not even an elementary knowledge of it.

Another point in his favour was a discovery

made at the spot where the body was found. Some profane and ribald words, also in French, had been scrawled in chalk on the door and doorsill, being in the nature of a coarse defiance to the police to find the assassin, and experts in handwriting who were called testified unanimously that Burwell, who wrote a refined, scholarly hand, could never have formed those misshapen words.

Furthermore, at the time of his arrest no evidence was found on the clothes or person of Burwell, nothing in the nature of bruises or bloodstains that would tend to implicate him in the crime. The outcome of the matter was that he was honourably discharged by the coroner's jury, who were unanimous in declaring him innocent, and who brought in a verdict that the unfortunate woman had come to her death at the hand of some person or persons unknown.

On visiting my patient late on the afternoon of the second day I saw that his case was very grave, and I at once instructed the nurses and attendants to prepare for an operation. The man's life depended upon my being able to extract the bullet, and the chance of doing this was very small. Mr. Burwell realized that his condition was critical, and, beckoning me to him, told me that he wished to make a statement he felt might be his last. He spoke with agitation which was increased by an unforeseen happening. For just then a servant entered the room and whispered to me that there was a gentleman downstairs who insisted upon seeing me, and who urged business of great importance. This message the sick man overheard, and lifting himself with an effort, he said excitedly: "Tell me, is he a tall man with glasses?"

The servant hesitated.

"I knew it; you cannot deceive me; that man will haunt me to my grave. Send him away, doctor; I beg of you not to see him."

Humouring my patient, I sent word to the stranger that I could not see him, but, in an undertone, instructed the servant to say that the man might call at my office the next morning. Then, turning to Burwell, I begged him to compose himself and save his strength for the ordeal awaiting him.

"No, no," he said, "I need my strength now to tell you what you must know to find the truth. You are the only man who has understood that there has been some terrible influence at work in my life. You are the only man competent to study out what that influence is, and I have made provision in my will that you shall do so after I am gone. I know that you will heed my wishes?"

The intense sadness of his eyes made my heart sink; I could only grip his hand and remain silent.

"Thank you; I was sure I might count on your devotion. Now, tell me, doctor, you have examined me carefully, have you not?"

I nodded.

"In every way known to medical science?"

I nodded again.

"And have you found anything wrong with me, — I mean, besides this bullet, anything abnormal?"

"As I have told you, your eyesight is defective; I should like to examine your eyes more thoroughly when you are better."

"I shall never be better; besides it isn't my eyes; I mean myself, my soul, — you haven't found anything wrong there?"

"Certainly not; the whole city knows the beauty of your character and your life."

"Tut, tut; the city knows nothing. For ten years I have lived so much with the poor that people have almost forgotten my previous active life when I was busy with money-making and happy in my home. But there is a man out West, whose head is white and whose heart is heavy, who has not forgotten, and there is a woman in London, a silent, lonely woman, who has not forgotten. The man was my partner, poor Jack Evelyth; the woman was my wife. How can a man be so cursed, doctor, that his love and friendship bring only misery to those who share it? How can it be that one who has in his heart only good thoughts can be constantly under the shadow of evil? This charge of murder is only one of several cases in my life where, through no fault of mine, the shadow of guilt has been cast upon me.

"Years ago, when my wife and I were perfectly happy, a child was born to us, and a few months later, when it was only a tender, helpless little thing that its mother loved with all her heart, it was strangled in its cradle, and we never knew who strangled it, for the deed was done one night when there was absolutely no one in the house but my wife and myself. There was no doubt about the crime, for there on the tiny neck were the finger marks where some cruel hand had closed until life went.

"Then a few years later, when my partner and I were on the eve of fortune, our advance was set back by the robbery of our safe. Some one opened it in the night, someone who knew the combination, for it was the work of no burglar, and yet there were only two persons in the world who knew that combination, my partner and myself. I tried to be brave when these things happened, but as my life went on it seemed more and more as if some curse were on me.

"Eleven years ago I went abroad with my wife and daughter. Business took me to Paris, and I left the ladies in London, expecting to have them join me in a few days. But they never did join me, for the curse was on me still, and before I had been forty-eight hours in the French capital something happened that completed the wreck of my life. It doesn't seem possible, does it, that a simple white card with some words scrawled on it in purple ink could effect a man's undoing? And yet that was my fate. The card was given me by a beautiful woman with eyes like stars. She is dead long ago, and why she wished to harm me I never knew. You must find that out.

"You see I did not know the language of the country, and, wishing to have the words translated, — surely that was natural enough, — I showed the card to others. But no one would tell me what it meant. And, worse than that, wherever I showed it, and to whatever person, there evil came upon me quickly. I was driven from one hotel after another; an old acquaintance turned his back on me; I was arrested and thrown into prison; I was ordered to leave the country."

The sick man paused for a moment in his weakness, but with an effort forced himself to continue: —

"When I went back to London, sure of comfort in the love of my wife, she too, on seeing the card, drove me from her with cruel words. And when finally, in deepest despair, I returned to New York, dear old Jack, the friend of a life-time, broke with me when I showed him what was written. What the words were I do not know, and suppose no one will ever know, for the ink has faded these many years. You will find the card in my safe with other papers. But I want you, when I am gone, to find out the mystery of my life; and — and — about my fortune, that must be held until you have decided. There is no one who needs my money as much as the poor in this city, and I have bequeathed it to them unless "

In an agony of mind, Mr. Burwell struggled to go on, I soothing and encouraging him.

"Unless you find what I am afraid to think, but — but — yes, I must say it, — that I have not been a good man, as the world thinks, but have — O doctor, if you find that I have unknowingly harmed any human being, I want that person, or these persons, to have my fortune. Promise that."

Seeing the wild light in Burwell's eyes, and the fever that was burning him, I gave the promise asked of me, and the sick man sank back calmer.

A little later, the nurse and attendants came for the operation. As they were about to administer the ether, Burwell pushed them from him, and insisted on having brought to his bedside an iron box from the safe.

"The card is here," he said, laying his trembling hand upon the box, "you will remember your promise!"

Those were his last words, for he did not survive the operation.

Early the next morning I received this message: "The stranger of yesterday begs to see you"; and presently a gentleman of fine presence and strength of face, a tall, dark-complexioned man wearing glasses, was shown into the room.

"Mr. Burwell is dead, is he not?" were his first words.

"Who told you?"

"No one told me, but I know it, and I thank God for it."

There was something in the stranger's intense earnestness that convinced me of his right to speak thus, and I listened attentively.

"That you may have confidence in the statement I am about to make, I will first tell you who I am"; and he handed me a card that caused me to lift my eyes in wonder, for it bore a very great name, that of one of Europe's most famous savants.

"You have done me much honour, sir," I said with respectful inclination.

"On the contrary you will oblige me by considering me in your debt, and by never revealing my connection with this wretched man. I am moved to speak partly from considerations of human justice, largely in the interest of medical science. It is right for me to tell you, doctor, that your patient was beyond question the Water Street assassin."

"Impossible!" I cried.

"You will not say so when I have finished my story, which takes me back to Paris, to the time, eleven years ago, when this man was making his first visit to the French capital."

"The mysterious card!" I exclaimed.

"Ah, he has told you of his experience, but not of what befell the night before, when he first met my sister."

"Your sister?"

"Yes, it was she who gave him the card, and, in trying to befriend him, made him suffer. She was in ill health at the time, so much so that we had left our native India for extended journeyings. Alas! we delayed too long, for my sister died in New York, only a few weeks later, and I honestly believe her taking off was hastened by anxiety inspired by this man."

"Strange," I murmured, "how the life of a simple New York merchant could become entangled with that of a great lady of the East."

"Yet so it was. You must know that my sister's condition was due mainly to an over fondness for certain occult investigations, from which I had vainly tried to dissuade her. She had once befriended some adepts, who, in return, had taught her things about the soul she had better have left unlearned. At various times while with her I had seen strange things happen, but I never realized what unearthly powers were in her until that night in Paris. We were returning from a drive in the Bois; it was about ten o'clock, and the city lay beautiful around us as Paris looks on a perfect summer's night. Suddenly my sister gave a cry of pain and put her hand to her heart. Then, changing from French to the language of our country, she explained to me quickly that something frightful was taking place there, where she pointed her finger across the river, that we must go to the place at once — the driver must lash his horses — every second was precious.

"So affected was I by her intense conviction, and such confidence had I in my sister's wisdom, that I did not oppose her, but told the man to drive as she directed. The carriage fairly flew across the bridge, down the Boulevard St. Germain, then to the left, threading its way through the narrow streets that lie along the Seine. This way and that, straight ahead here, a turn there, she directing our course, never hesitating, as if drawn by some unseen power, and always urging the driver on to greater speed. Finally, we came to a black-mouthed, evil-looking alley, so narrow and roughly paved that the carriage could scarcely advance.

"'Come on!' my sister cried, springing to the ground; 'we will go on foot, we are nearly there. Thank God, we may yet be in time.'

"No one was in sight as we hurried along the dark alley, and scarcely a light was visible, but presently a smothered scream broke the silence, and, touching my arm, my sister exclaimed: —

"'There, draw your weapon, quick, and take the man at any cost!'

"So swiftly did everything happen after that that I hardly know my actions, but a few minutes later I held pinioned in my arms a man whose blows and writhings had been all in vain; for you must know that much exercise in the jungle had made me strong of limb. As soon as I had made the fellow fast I looked down and found moaning on the ground a poor woman, who explained with tears and broken words that the man had been in the very act of strangling her. Searching him I found a long-bladed knife of curious shape, and keen as a razor, which had been brought for what horrible purpose you may perhaps divine.

"Imagine my surprise, on dragging the man back to the carriage, to find, instead of the ruffianly assassin I expected, a gentleman as far as could be judged from face and manner. Fine eyes, white hands, careful speech, all the signs of refinement and the dress of a man of means.

"'How can this be?' I said to my sister in our own tongue as we drove away, I holding my prisoner on the opposite seat where he sat silent.

"'It is a *kulos*-man,' she said, shivering, 'it is a fiend-soul. There are a few such in the whole world, perhaps two or three in all.'

"'But he has a good face.'

"'You have not seen his real face yet; I will show it to you, presently.'

"In the strangeness of these happenings and the still greater strangeness of my sister's words, I had all but lost the power of wonder. So we sat without further word until the carriage stopped at the little château we had taken near the Parc Monteau.

"I could never properly describe what happened that night; my knowledge of these things is too limited. I simply obeyed my sister in all that she directed, and kept my eyes on this man as no hawk ever watched its prey. She began by questioning him, speaking in a kindly tone which I could ill understand. He seemed embarrassed, dazed, and professed to have no knowledge of what had occurred, or how he had come where we found him. To all my inquiries as to the woman or the crime he shook his head blankly, and thus aroused my wrath.

"'Be not angry with him, brother; he is not lying, it is the other soul.'

"She asked him about his name and country, and he replied without hesitation that he was Richard Burwell, a merchant from New York, just arrived in Paris, travelling for pleasure in Europe with his wife and daughter. This seemed reasonable, for the man spoke English, and, strangely enough, seemed to have no knowledge of French, although we both remember hearing him speak French to the woman.

"'There is no doubt,' my sister said, 'It is indeed a *kulos*-man; It knows that I am here, that I am Its master. Look, look!' she cried sharply, at the same time putting her eyes so close to the man's face that their fierce light seemed to burn into him. What power she exercised I do not know, nor whether some words she spoke, unintelligible to me, had to do with what followed, but instantly there came over this man, this pleasant-looking, respectable American citizen, such a change as is not made by death worms gnawing in a grave. Now there was a fiend grovelling at her feet, a foul, sin-stained fiend.

"'Now you see the demon-soul,' said my sister. 'Watch It writhe and struggle; it has served me well, brother, sayest thou not so, the lore I gained from our wise men?'

"The horror of what followed chilled my blood; nor would I trust my memory were it not that there remained and still remains plain proof of all that I affirm. This hideous creature, dwarfed, crouching, devoid of all resemblance to the man we had but now beheld, chattering to us in curious old-time French, poured out such horrid blasphemy as would have blanched the cheek of Satan, and made recital of such evil deeds as never mortal ear gave heed to. And as she willed my sister checked It or allowed It to go on. What it all meant was more than I could tell. To me it seemed as if these tales of wickedness had no connection with our modern life, or with the world around us, and so I judged presently from what my sister said.

"'Speak of the later time, since thou wast in this clay.'

"Then I perceived that the creature came to things of which I knew: It spoke of New York, of a wife, a child, a friend. It told of strangling the child, of robbing the friend; and was going on to tell God knows what other horrid deeds when my sister stopped It.

"'Stand as thou didst in killing the little babe, stand, stand!' and once more she spoke some words unknown to me. Instantly the demon sprang forward, and, bending Its clawlike hands, clutched them around some little throat that was not there, — but I could see it in my mind. And the look on its face was a blackest glimpse of hell.

"'And now stand as thou didst in robbing the friend, stand, stand'; and again came the unknown words, and again the fiend obeyed.

"'These we will take for future use,' said my sister. And bidding me watch the creature carefully until she should return, she left the room, and, after none too short an absence, returned bearing a black box that was an apparatus for photography, and something more besides, — some newer, stranger kind of photography that she had learned. Then, on a strangely fashioned card, a transparent white card, composed of many layers of finest Oriental paper, she took the pictures of the creature in those two creeping poses. And when it all was done, the card seemed as white as before, and empty of all meaning until one held it up and examined it intently. Then the pictures showed.

And between the two there was a third picture, which somehow seemed to show, at the same time, two faces in one, two souls, my sister said, the kindly visaged man we first had seen, and then the fiend.

"Now my sister asked for pen and ink and I gave her my pocket pen which was filled with purple ink. Handing this to the *kulos*-man she bade him write under the first picture: 'Thus I killed my babe.' And under the second picture: 'Thus I robbed my friend.' And under the third, the one that was between the other two: 'This is the soul of Richard Burwell.' An odd thing about this writing was that it was in the same old French the creature had used in speech, and yet Burwell knew no French.

"My sister was about to finish with the creature when a new idea took her, and she said, looking at It as before: — 'Of all thy crimes which one is the worst? Speak, I command thee!'

"Then the fiend told how once It had killed every soul in a house of holy women and buried the bodies in a cellar under a heavy door.

"Where was the house?'

"'At No. 19 Rue Picpus, next to the old graveyard.'

"'And when was this?'

"Here the fiend seemed to break into fierce rebellion, writhing on the floor with hideous contortions, and pouring forth words that meant nothing to me, but seemed to reach my sister's understanding, for she interrupted from time to time, with quick, stern words that finally brought It to subjection.

"'Enough,' she said, 'I know all,' and then she spoke some words again, her eyes fixed as before, and the reverse change came. Before us stood once more the honest-looking, fine-appearing gentleman, Richard Burwell, of New York.

"'Excuse me, madame,' he said, awkwardly, but with deference; 'I must have dosed a little. I am not myself to-night.'

"'No,' said my sister, 'you have not been yourself to-night.'

"A little later I accompanied the man to the Continental Hotel, where he was stopping, and, returning to my sister, I talked with her until late into the night. I was alarmed to see that she was wrought to a nervous tension that augured ill for her health. I urged her to sleep, but she would not.

"'No,' she said, 'think of the awful responsibility that rests upon me.' And then she went on with her strange theories and explanations, of which I understood only that here was a power for evil more terrible than a pestilence, menacing all humanity.

"'Once in many cycles it happens,' she said, 'that a *kulos*-soul pushes itself within the body of a new-born child, when the pure soul waiting to enter is delayed. Then the two live together through that life, and this hideous principle of evil has a chance upon the earth. It is my will, as I feel it my duty, to see this poor man again. The chances are that he will never know us, for the shock of this night to his normal soul is so great as to wipe out memory.'

"The next evening, about the same hour, my sister insisted that I should go with her to the *Folies Bergère*, a concert garden, none too well frequented, and when I remonstrated, she said: 'I must go, — It is there,' and the words sent a shiver through me.

"We drove to this place, and passing into the garden, presently discovered Richard Burwell seated at a little table, enjoying the scene of pleasure, which was plainly new to him. My sister hesitated a moment what to do, and then, leaving my arm, she advanced to the table and dropped before Burwell's eyes the card she had prepared. A moment later, with a look of pity on her beautiful face, she rejoined me and we went away. It was plain he did not know us."

To so much of the savant's strange recital I had listened with absorbed interest, though without a word, but now I burst in with questions.

"What was your sister's idea in giving Burwell the card?" I asked.

"It was in the hope that she might make the man understand his terrible condition, that is, teach the pure soul to know its loathsome companion."

"And did her effort succeed?"

"Alas! it did not; my sister's purpose was defeated by the man's inability to see the pictures that were plain to every other eye. It is impossible for the *kulos*-man to know his own degradation."

"And yet this man has for years been leading a most exemplary life?"

My visitor shook his head. "I grant you there has been improvement, due largely to experiments I have conducted upon him according to my sister's wishes. But the fiend soul was never driven out. It grieves me to tell you, doctor, that not only was this man the Water Street assassin, but he was the mysterious murderer, the long-sought-for mutilator of women, whose red crimes have baffled the police of Europe and America for the past ten years."

"You know this," said I, starting up, "and yet did not denounce him?"

"It would have been impossible to prove such a charge, and besides, I had made oath to my sister that I would use the man only for these soul-experiments. What are his crimes compared with the great secret of knowledge I am now able to give the world?"

"A secret of knowledge?"

"Yes," said the savant, with intense earnestness, "I may tell you now, doctor, what the whole world will know, ere long, that it is possible to compel every living person to reveal the innermost secrets of his or her life, so long as memory remains, for memory is only the power of producing in the brain material pictures that may be projected externally by the thought rays and made to impress themselves upon the photographic plate, precisely as ordinary pictures do."

"You mean," I exclaimed, "that you can photograph the two principles of good and evil that exist in us?"

"Exactly that. The great truth of a dual soul existence, that was dimly apprehended by one of your Western novelists, has been demonstrated by me in the laboratory with my camera. It is my purpose, at the proper time, to entrust this precious knowledge to a chosen few who will perpetuate it and use it worthily."

"Wonderful, wonderful!" I cried, "and now tell me, if you will, about the house on the Rue Picpus. Did you ever visit the place?"

"We did, and found that no buildings had stood there for fifty years, so we did not pursue the search." [1]

"And the writing on the card, have you any memory of it, for Burwell told me that the words have faded?"

"I have something better than that; I have a photograph of both card and writing, which my sister was careful to take. I had a notion that the ink in my pocket pen would fade, for it was a poor affair. This photograph I will bring you to-morrow."

"Bring it to Burwell's house," I said.

*****

The next morning the stranger called as agreed upon.

"Here is the photograph of the card," he said.

"And here is the original card," I answered, breaking the seal of the envelope I had taken from Burwell's iron box. "I have waited for your arrival to look at it. Yes, the writing has indeed vanished; the card seems quite blank."

"Not when you hold it this way," said the stranger, and as he tipped the card I saw such a horrid revelation as I can never forget. In an instant I realized how the shock of seeing that card had been too great for the soul of wife or friend to bear. In these pictures was the secret of a cursed life. The resemblance to Burwell was unmistakable, the proof against him was overwhelming. In looking upon that piece of pasteboard the wife had seen a crime which the mother could never forgive, the partner had seen a crime which the friend could never forgive. Think of a loved face suddenly melting before your eyes into a grinning skull, then into a mass of putrefaction, then into the ugliest fiend of hell, leering at you, distorted with all the marks of vice and shame. That is what I saw, that is what they had seen!

"Let us lay these two cards in the coffin," said my companion impressively, "we have done what we could."

Eager to be rid of the hateful piece of pasteboard (for who could say that the curse was not still clinging about it?), I took the strange man's arm, and together we advanced into the adjoining room where the body lay. I had seen Burwell as he breathed his last, and knew that there had been a peaceful look on his face as he died. But now, as we laid the two white cards on the still, breast, the savant suddenly touched my arm, and pointing to the dead man's face, now frightfully distorted, whispered: — "See, even in death It followed him. Let us close the coffin quickly."

*****

[1] Years later, some workmen in Paris, making excavations in the Rue Picpus, came upon a heavy door buried under a mass of debris, under an old cemetery. On lifting the door they found a vault-like chamber in which were a number of female skeletons, and graven on the walls were blasphemous

words written in French, which experts declared dated from fully two hundred years before. They also declared this handwriting identical with that found on the door at the Water Street murder in New York. Thus we may deduce a theory of fiend reincarnation; for it would seem clear, almost to the point of demonstration, that this murder of the seventeenth century was the work of the same evil soul that killed the poor woman on Water Street towards the end of the nineteenth century.

II. The Great Valdez Sapphir — (Anonymous)

I know more about it than anyone else in the world, its present owner not excepted. I can give its whole history, from the Cingalese who found it, the Spanish adventurer who stole it, the cardinal who bought it, the Pope who graciously accepted it, the favoured son of the Church who received it, the gay and giddy duchess who pawned it, down to the eminent prelate who now holds it in trust as a family heirloom.

It will occupy a chapter to itself in my forthcoming work on "Historic Stones," where full details of its weight, size, colour, and value may be found. At present I am going to relate an incident in its history which, for obvious reasons, will not be published — which, in fact, I trust the reader will consider related in strict confidence.

I had never seen the stone itself when I began to write about it, and it was not till one evening last spring, while staying with my nephew, Sir Thomas Acton, that I came within measurable distance of it. A dinner party was impending, and, at my instigation, the Bishop of Northchurch and Miss Panton, his daughter and heiress, were among the invited guests.

The dinner was a particularly good one, I remember that distinctly. In fact, I felt myself partly responsible for it, having engaged the new cook — a talented young Italian, pupil of the admirable old *chef* at my club. We had gone over the *menu* carefully together, with a result refreshing in its novelty, but not so daring as to disturb the minds of the innocent country guests who were bidden thereto.

The first spoonful of soup was reassuring, and I

looked to the end of the table to exchange a congratulatory glance with Leta. What was amiss? No response. Her pretty face was flushed, her smile constrained, she was talking with quite unnecessary *empressement* to her neighbour, Sir Harry Landor, though Leta is one of those few women who understand the importance of letting a man settle down tranquilly and with an undisturbed mind to the business of dining, allowing no topic of serious interest to come on before the *relevés*, and reserving mere conversational brilliancy for the *entremets*.

Guests all right? No disappointments? I had gone through the list with her, selecting just the right people to be asked to meet the Landors, our new neighbours. Not a mere cumbrous county gathering, nor yet a showy imported party from town, but a skillful blending of both. Had anything happened already? I had been late for dinner and missed the arrivals in the drawing-room. It was Leta's fault. She has got into a way of coming into my room and putting the last touches to my toilet. I let her, for I am doubtful of myself nowadays after many years' dependence on the best of valets. Her taste is generally beyond dispute, but to-day she had indulged in a feminine vagary that provoked me and made me late for dinner.

"Are you going to wear your sapphire, Uncle Paul!" she cried in a tone of dismay. "Oh, why not the ruby?"

"You *would* have your way about the table decorations," I gently reminded her. "With that service of Crown Derby *repoussé* and orchids, the ruby would look absolutely barbaric. Now if you would have had the Limoges set, white candles, and a yellow silk centre — "

"Oh, but — I'm *so* disappointed — I wanted the bishop to see your ruby — or one of your engraved gems — "

"My dear, it is on the bishop's account I put this on. You know his daughter is heiress of the great Valdez sapphire — "

"Of course she is, and when he has the charge of a stone three times as big as yours, what's the use of wearing it? The ruby, dear Uncle Paul, *please!*"

She was desperately in earnest I could see, and considering the obligations which I am supposed to be under to her and Tom, it was but a little matter to yield, but it involved a good deal of extra trouble. Studs, sleeve-links, watch-guard, all carefully selected to go with the sapphire, had to be changed, the emerald which I chose as a compromise requiring more florid accompaniments of a deeper tone of gold; and the dinner hour struck as I replaced my jewel case, the one relic left me of a once handsome fortune, in my fireproof safe.

The emerald looked very well that evening, however. I kept my eyes upon it for comfort when Miss Panton proved trying.

She was a lean, yellow, dictatorial young person with no conversation. I spoke of her father's celebrated sapphires. "*My* sapphires," she amended sourly; "though I am legally debarred from making any profitable use of them." She furthermore informed me that she viewed them as useless gauds, which ought to be disposed of for the benefit of the heathen. I gave the subject up, and while she discoursed of the work of the Blue Ribbon Army among the Bosjesmans I tried to understand a certain dislocation in the arrangement of the table.

Surely we were more or less in number than we should be? Opposite side all right. Who was extra on ours? I leaned forward. Lady Landor on one side of Tom, on the other who? I caught glimpses of plumes pink and green nodding over a dinner plate, and beneath them a pink nose in a green visage with a nutcracker chin altogether unknown to me. A sharp gray eye shot a sideway glance down the table and caught me peeping, and I retreated, having only marked in addition two clawlike hands, with pointed ruffles and a mass of brilliant rings, making good play with a knife and fork. Who was she? At intervals a high acid voice could be heard addressing Tom, and a laugh that made me shudder; it had the quality of the scream of a bird of prey or the yell of a jackal. I had heard that sort of laugh before, and it always made me feel like a defenseless rabbit.

Every time it sounded I saw Leta's fan flutter more furiously and her manner grow more nervously animated. Poor dear girl! I never in all my recollection wished a dinner at an end so earnestly so as to assure her of my support and sympathy, though without the faintest conception why either should be required.

The ices at last. A *menu* card folded in two was laid beside me. I read it unobserved. "Keep the B. from joining us in the drawing-room." The B. — ? The bishop, of course. With pleasure. But why? And how? *That's* the question, never mind "why." Could I lure him into the library — the billiard room — the conservatory? I doubted it, and I doubted still more what I should do with him when I got him there.

The bishop is a grand and stately ecclesiastic of the mediæval type, broad-chested, deep-voiced, martial of bearing. I could picture him charging mace in hand at the head of his vassals, or delivering over a dissenter of the period to the rack and thumb-screw, but not pottering among rare editions, tall copies and Grolier bindings, nor condescending to a quiet cigar among the tree ferns and orchids. Leta must and should be obeyed, I swore, nevertheless, even if I were driven to lock the door in the fearless old fashion of a bygone day, and declare I'd shoot any man who left while a drop remained in the bottles.

The ladies were rising. The lady at the head of the line smirked and nodded her pink plumes coquettishly at Tom, while her hawk's eyes roved keen and predatory over us all. She stopped suddenly, creating a block and confusion.

"Ah, the dear bishop! *You* there, and I never saw you! You must come and have a nice long chat presently. By-by — !" She shook her fan at him over my shoulder and tripped on. Leta, passing me last, gave me a look of profound despair.

"Lady Carwitchet!" somebody exclaimed. "I couldn't believe my eyes."

"Thought she was dead or in penal servitude. Never should have expected to see her *here*," said someone else behind me confidentially.

"What Carwitchet? Not the mother of the Carwitchet who — "

"Just so. The Carwitchet who — " Tom assented with a shrug. "We needn't go farther, as she's my guest. Just my luck. I met them at Buxton, thought them uncommonly good company — in fact, Carwitchet laid me under a great obligation about a horse I was nearly let in for buying — and gave them a general invitation here, as one does, you know. Never expected her to turn up with her luggage this afternoon just before dinner, to stay a week, or a fortnight if Carwitchet can join her." A groan of sympathy ran round the table. "It can't be helped. I've told you this just to show that I shouldn't have asked you here to meet this sort of people of my own free will; but, as it is, please say no more about them." The subject was not dropped by any means, and I took care that it should not be. At our end of the table one story after another went buzzing round — *sotto voce*, out of deference to Tom — but perfectly audible.

"Carwitchet? Ah, yes. Mixed up in that Rawlings divorce case, wasn't he? A bad lot. Turned out of the Dragoon Guards for cheating at cards, or picking pockets, or something — remember the row at the Cerulean Club? Scandalous exposure — and that forged letter business — oh, that was the mother — prosecution hushed up somehow. Ought to be serving her fourteen years — and that business of poor Farrars, the banker — got hold of some of his secrets and blackmailed him till he blew his brains out — "

It was so exciting that I clean forgot the bishop, till a low gasp at my elbow startled me. He was lying back in his chair, his mighty shaven jowl a ghastly white, his fierce imperious eyebrows drooping limp over his fishlike eyes, his splendid figure shrunk and contracted. He was trying with a shaken hand to pour out wine. The decanter clattered against the glass and the wine spilled on the cloth.

"I'm afraid you find the room too warm. Shall we go into the library?"

He rose hastily and followed me like a lamb.

He recovered himself once we got into the hall, and affably rejected all my proffers of brandy and soda — medical advice — everything else my limited experience could suggest. He only demanded his carriage "directly" and that Miss Panton should be summoned forthwith.

I made the best use I could of the time left me.

"I'm uncommonly sorry you do not feel equal to staying a little longer, my lord. I counted on showing you my few trifles of precious stones, the salvage from the wreck of my possessions. Nothing in comparison with your own collection."

The bishop clasped his hand over his heart. His breath came short and quick.

"A return of that dizziness," he explained with a faint smile. "You are thinking of the Valdez sapphire, are you not? Some day," he went on with forced composure, "I may have the pleasure of showing it to you. It is at my banker's just now."

Miss Panton's steps were heard in the hall. "You are well known as a connoisseur, Mr. Acton," he went on hurriedly. "Is your collection valuable? If so, *keep it safe; don' trust a ring off your hand, or the key of your jewel-case out of your pocket till the house is clear again.*" The words rushed from his lips in an impetuous whisper, he gave me a meaning glance, and departed with his daughter. I went back to the drawing-room, my head swimming with bewilderment.

"What! The dear bishop gone!" screamed Lady Carwitchet from the central ottoman where she sat, surrounded by most of the gentlemen, all apparently well entertained by her conversation. "And I wanted to talk over old times with him so badly.

His poor wife was my greatest friend. Mira Montanaro, daughter of the great banker, you know. It's not possible that that miserable little prig is my poor Mira's girl. The heiress of all the Montanaros in a black-lace gown worth twopence! When I think of her mother's beauty and her toilets! Does she ever wear the sapphires? Has anyone ever seen her in them? Eleven large stones in a lovely antique setting, and the great Valdez sapphire — worth thousands and thousands — for the pendant." No one replied. "I wanted to get a rise out of the bishop tonight. It used to make him so mad when I wore this."

She fumbled among the laces at her throat, and clawed out a pendant that hung to a velvet band around her neck. I fairly gasped when she removed her hand. A sapphire of irregular shape flashed out its blue lightning on us. Such a stone! A true, rich, cornflower blue even by that wretched artificial light, with soft velvety depths of colour and dazzling clearness of tint in its lights and shades — a stone to remember! I stretched out my hand involuntarily, but Lady Carwitchet drew back with a coquettish squeal. "No! no! You mustn't look any closer. Tell me what you think of it now. Isn't it pretty?"

"Superb!" was all I could ejaculate, staring at the azure splendour of that miraculous jewel in a sort of trance.

She gave a shrill cackling laugh of mockery.

"The great Mr. Acton taken in by a bit of Palais Royal gimcrackery! What an advertisement for Bogaerts et Cie! They are perfect artists in frauds. Don't you remember their stand at the first Paris Exhibition? They had imitations there of every celebrated stone; but I never expected anything made by man could delude Mr. Acton, never!" And she went off into another mocking cackle, and all the idiots round her haw-hawed knowingly, as if they had seen the joke all along. I was too bewildered to reply, which was on the whole lucky. "I suppose I musn't tell why I came to give quite a big sum in francs for this?" she went on, tapping her closed lips with her closed fan, and cocking her eye at us all like a parrot wanting to be coaxed to talk. "It's a queer story."

I didn't want to hear her anecdote, especially as I saw she wanted to tell it. What I *did* want was to see that pendant again. She had thrust it back among her laces, only the loop which held it to the velvet being visible. It was set with three small sapphires, and even from a distance I clearly made them out to be imitations, and poor ones. I felt a queer thrill of self-mistrust. Was the large stone no better? Could I, even for an instant, have been dazzled by a sham, and a sham of that quality? The events of the evening had flurried and confused me. I wished to think them over in quiet. I would go to bed.

My rooms at the Manor are the best in the house. Leta will have it so. I must explain their position for a reason to be understood later. My bedroom is in the southeast angle of the house; it opens on one side into a sitting-room in the east corridor, the rest of which is taken up by the suite of rooms occupied by Tom and Leta; and on the other side into my bathroom, the first room in the south corridor where the principal guest chambers are, to one of which it was originally the dressing-room. Passing this room I noticed a couple of housemaids preparing it for the night, and discovered with a shiver that Lady Carwitchet was to be my next-door neighbour. It gave me a turn.

The bishop's strange warning must have unnerved me. I was perfectly safe from her ladyship. The disused door into her room was locked, and the key safe on the housekeeper's bunch. It was also undiscoverable on her side, the recess in which it stood being completely filled by a large wardrobe. On my side hung a thick sound-proof *portière*. Nevertheless, I resolved not to use that room while she inhabited the next one. I removed my possessions, fastened the door of communication with my bedroom and dragged a heavy ottoman across it.

Then I stowed away my emerald in my strongbox. It is built into the wall of my sitting-room, and masked by the lower part of an old carved oak bureau. I put away even the rings I wore habitually, keeping out only an inferior cat's-eye for workaday wear. I had just made all safe when Leta tapped at the door and came in to wish me good night. She looked flushed and harassed and ready to cry. "Uncle Paul," she began, "I want you to go up to town at once, and stay away till I send for you."

"My dear — !" I was too amazed to expostulate.

"We've got a — a pestilence among us," she declared, her foot tapping the ground angrily, "and the least we can do is to go into quarantine. Oh, I'm so sorry and so ashamed! The poor bishop! I'll take good care that no one else shall meet that woman here. You did your best for me, Uncle Paul, and managed admirably, but it was all no use. I hoped against hope that what between the dusk of the drawing-room before dinner, and being put at opposite ends of the table, we might get through without a meeting — "

"But, my dear, explain. Why shouldn't the bishop and Lady Carwitchet meet? Why is it worse for him than anyone else?"

"Why? I thought everybody had heard of that dreadful wife of his who nearly broke his heart. If he married her for her money it served him right, but Lady Landor says she was very handsome and really in love with him at first. Then Lady Carwitchet got hold of her and led her into all sorts of mischief. She left her husband — he was only a rector with a country living in those days — and went to live in town, got into a horrid fast set, and made herself notorious. You *must* have heard of her."

"I heard of her sapphires, my dear. But I was in Brazil at the time."

"I wish you had been at home. You might have found her out. She was furious because her husband refused to let her wear the great Valdez sapphire. It had been in the Montanaro family for some generations, and her father settled it first on her and then on her little girl — the bishop being trustee. He felt obliged to take away the little girl, and send her off to be brought up by some old aunts in the country, and he locked up the sapphire. Lady Carwitchet tells as a splendid joke how they got the copy made in Paris, and it did just as well for the people to stare at. No wonder the bishop hates the very name of the stone."

"How long will she stay here?" I asked dismally.

"Till Lord Carwitchet can come and escort her to Paris to visit some American friends. Goodness knows when that will be! Do go up to town, Uncle Paul!"

I refused indignantly. The very least I could do was to stand by my poor young relatives in their troubles and help them through. I did so. I wore that inferior cat's eye for six weeks!

It is a time I cannot think of even now without a shudder. The more I saw of that terrible old woman the more I detested her, and we saw a very great deal of her. Leta kept her word, and neither accepted nor gave invitations all that time. We were cut off from all society but that of old General Fairford, who would go anywhere and meet anyone to get a rubber after dinner; the doctor, a sporting widower; and the Duberlys, a giddy, rather rackety young couple who had taken the Dower House for a year. Lady Carwitchet seemed perfectly content. She revelled in the soft living and good fare of the Manor House, the drives in Leta's big barouche, and Domenico's dinners, as one to whom short commons were not unknown. She had a hungry way of grabbing and grasping at everything she could — the shillings she won at whist, the best fruit at dessert, the postage stamps in the library inkstand — that was infinitely suggestive. Sometimes I could have pitied her, she was so greedy, so spiteful, so friendless. She always made me think of some wicked old pirate putting into a peaceful port to provision and repair his battered old hulk, obliged to live on friendly terms with the natives, but his piratical old nostrils asniff for plunder and his piratical old soul longing to be off marauding once more. When would that be? Not till the arrival in Paris of her distinguished American friends, of whom we heard a great deal. "Charming people, the Bokums of Chicago, the American branch of the English Beauchamps, you know!" They seemed to be taking an unconscionable time to get there. She would have insisted on being driven over to Northchurch to call at the palace, but that the bishop was understood to be holding confirmations at the other end of the diocese.

I was alone in the house one afternoon sitting by my window, toying with the key of my safe, and wondering whether I dare treat myself to a peep at my treasures, when a suspicious movement in the park below caught my attention. A black figure certainly dodged from behind one tree to the next, and then into the shadow of the park paling instead of keeping to the footpath. It looked queer. I caught up my field glass and marked him at one point where he was bound to come into the open for a few steps. He crossed the strip of turf with giant strides and got into cover again, but not quick enough to prevent me recognizing him. It was — great heavens! — the bishop! In a soft hat pulled over his forehead, with a long cloak and a big stick he looked like a poacher.

Guided by some mysterious instinct I hurried to meet him. I opened the conservatory door, and in he rushed like a hunted rabbit. Without explanation I led him up the wide staircase to my room, where he dropped into a chair and wiped his face.

"You are astonished, Mr. Acton," he panted. "I will explain directly. Thanks." He tossed off the glass of brandy I had poured out without waiting for the qualifying soda, and looked better.

"I am in serious trouble. You can help me. I've had a shock to-day — a grievous shock." He stopped and tried to pull himself together. "I must trust you implicitly, Mr. Acton, I have no choice. Tell me what you think of this." He drew a case from his breast pocket and opened it. "I promised you should see the Valdez sapphire. Look there!"

The Valdez sapphire! A great big shining lump of blue crystal — flawless and of perfect colour — that was all. I took it up, breathed on it, drew out my magnifier, looked at it in one light and another. What was wrong with it? I could not say. Nine experts out of ten would undoubtedly have pronounced the stone genuine. I, by virtue of some mysterious instinct that has hitherto always guided me aright, was the unlucky tenth. I looked at the bishop. His eyes met mine. There was no need of spoken word between us.

"Has Lady Carwitchet shown you her sapphire?" was his most unexpected question. "She has? Now, Mr. Acton, on your honour as a connoisseur and a gentleman, which of the two is the Valdez?"

"Not this one." I could say naught else.

"You were my last hope." He broke off, and dropped his face on his folded arms with a groan that shook the table on which he rested, while I stood dismayed at myself for having let so hasty a judgment escape me. He lifted a ghastly countenance to me. "She vowed she would see me ruined and disgraced. I made her my enemy by crossing some of her schemes once, and she never forgives. She will keep her word. I shall appear before the world as a fraudulent trustee. I can neither produce the valuable confided to my charge nor make the loss good. I have only an incredible story to tell," he dropped his head and groaned again. "Who will believe me?"

"I will, for one."

"Ah, you? Yes, you know her. She took my wife from me, Mr. Acton. Heaven only knows what the hold was that she had over poor Mira. She encouraged her to set me at defiance and eventually to leave me. She was answerable for all the scandalous folly and extravagance of poor Mira's life in Paris — spare me the telling of the story. She left her at last to die alone and uncared for. I reached my wife to find her dying of a fever from which Lady Carwitchet and her crew had fled. She was raving in delirium, and died without recognizing me. Some trouble she had been in which I must never know oppressed her. At the very last she roused from a long stupor and spoke to the nurse. 'Tell him to get the sapphire back — she stole it. She has robbed my child.' Those were her last words. The nurse understood no English, and treated them as wandering; but *I* heard them, and knew she was sane when she spoke."

"What did you do?"

"What could I? I saw Lady Carwitchet, who laughed at me, and defied me to make her confess or disgorge. I took the pendant to more than one eminent jeweller on pretense of having the setting seen to, and all have examined and admired without giving a hint of there being anything wrong. I allowed a celebrated mineralogist to see it; he gave no sign — "

"Perhaps they are right and we are wrong."

"No, no. Listen. I heard of an old Dutchman celebrated for his imitations. I went to him, and he told me at once that he had been allowed by Montanaro to copy the Valdez — setting and all — for the Paris Exhibition. I showed him this, and he claimed it for his own work at once, and pointed out his private mark upon it. You must take your magnifier to find it; a Greek Beta. He also told me that he had sold it to Lady Carwitchet more than a year ago."

"It is a terrible position."

"It is. My co-trustee died lately. I have never dared to have another appointed. I am bound to hand over the sapphire to my daughter on her marriage, if her husband consents to take the name of Montanaro."

The bishop's face was ghastly pale, and the moisture started on his brow. I racked my brain for some word of comfort.

"Miss Panton may never marry."

"But she will!" he shouted. "That is the blow that has been dealt me to-day. My chaplain — actually, my chaplain — tells me that he is going out as a temperance missionary to equatorial Africa, and has the assurance to add that he believes my daughter is not indisposed to accompany him!" His consummating wrath acted as a momentary stimulant. He sat upright, his eyes flashing and his brow thunderous. I felt for that chaplain. Then he collapsed miserably. "The sapphires will have to be produced, identified, revalued. How shall I come out of it? Think of the disgrace, the ripping up of old scandals! Even if I were to compound with Lady Carwitchet, the sum she hinted at was too monstrous. She wants more than my money. Help me, Mr. Acton! For the sake of your own family interest, help me!"

"I beg your pardon — family interests? I don't understand."

"If my daughter is childless, her next of kin is poor Marmaduke Panton, who is dying at Cannes, not married, or likely to marry; and failing him, your nephew, Sir Thomas Acton, succeeds."

My nephew Tom! Leta, or Leta's baby, might come to be the possible inheritor of the great Valdez sapphire! The blood rushed to my head as I looked at the great shining swindle before me. "What diabolic jugglery was at work when the exchange was made?" I demanded fiercely.

"It must have been on the last occasion of her wearing the sapphires in London. I ought never to have let her out of my sight."

"You must put a stop to Miss Panton's marriage in the first place," I pronounced as autocratically as he could have done himself.

"Not to be thought of," he admitted helplessly. "Mira has my force of character. She knows her rights, and she will have her jewels. I want you to take charge of the — thing for me. If it's in the house she'll make me produce it. She'll inquire at the banker's. If *you* have it we can gain time, if but for a day or two." He broke off. Carriage wheels were crashing on the gravel outside. We looked at one another in consternation. Flight was imperative. I hurried him downstairs and out of the conservatory just as the door-bell rang. I think we both lost our heads in the confusion. He shoved the case into my hands, and I pocketed it, without a thought of the awful responsibility I was incurring, and saw him disappear into the shelter of the friendly night.

When I think of what my feelings were that evening — of my murderous hatred of that smirking jesting Jezebel who sat opposite me at dinner, my wrathful indignation at the thought of the poor little expected heir defrauded ere his birth; of the crushing contempt I felt for myself and the bishop as a pair of witless idiots unable to see our way out of the dilemma; all this boiling and surging through my soul, I can only wonder — Domenico having given himself a holiday, and the kitchen-maid doing her worst and wickedest — that gout or jaundice did not put an end to this story at once.

"Uncle Paul!" Leta was looking her sweetest when she tripped into my room next morning. "I've news for you. She," pointing a delicate forefinger in the direction of the corridor, "is going! Her Bokums have reached Paris at last, and sent for her to join them at the Grand Hotel."

I was thunderstruck. The longed-for deliverance had but come to remove hopelessly and forever out of my reach Lady Carwitchet and the great Valdez sapphire.

"Why, aren't you overjoyed? I am. We are going to celebrate the event by a dinner-party. Tom's hospitable soul is vexed by the lack of entertainment we had provided for her. We must ask the Brownleys some day or other, and they will be delighted to meet anything in the way of a ladyship, or such smart folks as the Duberly-Parkers. Then we may as well have the Blomfields, and air that awful modern Sèvres dessert-service she gave us when we were married." I had no objection to make, and she went on, rubbing her soft cheek against my shoulder like the purring little cat she was: "Now I want you to do something to please me — and Mrs. Blomfield. She has set her heart on seeing your rubies, and though I know you hate her about as much as you do that Sèvres china — "

"What! Wear my rubies with that! I won't. I'll tell you what I will do, though. I've got some carbuncles as big as prize gooseberries, a whole set.

Then you have only to put those Bohemian glass vases and candelabra on the table, and let your gardener do his worst with his great forced, scentless, vulgar blooms, and we shall all be in keeping." Leta pouted. An idea struck me. "Or I'll do as you wish, on one condition. You get Lady Carwitchet to wear her big sapphire, and don't tell her I wish it."

I lived through the next few days as one in some evil dream. The sapphires, like twin spectres, haunted me day and night. Was ever man so tantalized? To hold the shadow and see the substance dangled temptingly within reach. The bishop made no sign of ridding me of my unwelcome charge, and the thought of what might happen in a case of burglary — fire — earthquake — made me start and tremble at all sorts of inopportune moments.

I kept faith with Leta, and reluctantly produced my beautiful rubies on the night of her dinner party. Emerging from my room I came full upon Lady Carwitchet in the corridor. She was dressed for dinner, and at her throat I caught the blue gleam of the great sapphire. Leta had kept faith with me. I don't know what I stammered in reply to her ladyship's remarks; my whole soul was absorbed in the contemplation of the intoxicating loveliness of the gem. *That* a Palais Royal deception! Incredible! My fingers twitched, my breath came short and fierce with the lust of possession. She must have seen the covetous glare in my eyes. A look of gratified spiteful complacency overspread her features, as she swept on ahead and descended the stairs before me. I followed her to the drawing-room door. She stopped suddenly, and murmuring something unintelligible hurried back again.

Everybody was assembled there that I expected

to see, with an addition. Not a welcome one by the look on Tom's face. He stood on the hearth-rug conversing with a great hulking, high-shouldered fellow, sallow-faced, with a heavy moustache and drooping eyelids, from the corners of which flashed out a sudden suspicious look as I approached, which lighted up into a greedy one as it rested on my rubies, and seemed unaccountably familiar to me, till Lady Carwitchet tripping past me exclaimed:

"He has come at last! My naughty, naughty boy! Mr. Acton, this is my son, Lord Carwitchet!"

I broke off short in the midst of my polite acknowledgments to stare blankly at her. The sapphire was gone! A great gilt cross, with a Scotch pebble like an acid drop, was her sole decoration.

"I had to put my pendant away," she explained confidentially; "the clasp had got broken somehow." I didn't believe a word.

Lord Carwitchet contributed little to the general entertainment at dinner, but fell into confidential talk with Mrs. Duberly-Parker. I caught a few unintelligible remarks across the table. They referred, I subsequently discovered, to the lady's little book on Northchurch races, and I recollected that the Spring Meeting was on, and to-morrow "Cup Day." After dinner there was great talk about getting up a party to go on General Fairford's drag. Lady Carwitchet was in ecstasies and tried to coax me into joining. Leta declined positively. Tom accepted sulkily.

The look in Lord Carwitchet's eye returned to my mind as I locked up my rubies that night. It made him look so like his mother! I went round my fastenings with unusual care. Safe and closets and desk and doors, I tried them all. Coming at last to the bathroom, it opened at once. It was the housemaid's doing. She had evidently taken advantage of my having abandoned the room to give it "a thorough spring cleaning," and I anathematized her. The furniture was all piled together and veiled with sheets, the carpet and felt curtain were gone, there were new brooms about. As I peered around, a voice close at my ear made me jump — Lady Carwitchet's!

"I tell you I have nothing, not a penny! I shall have to borrow my train fare before I can leave this. They'll be glad enough to lend it."

Not only had the *portière* been removed, but the door behind it had been unlocked and left open for convenience of dusting behind the wardrobe. I might as well have been in the bedroom.

"Don't tell me," I recognized Carwitchet's growl. "You've not been here all this time for nothing. You've been collecting for a Kilburn cot or getting subscriptions for the distressed Irish landlords. I know you. Now I'm not going to see myself ruined for the want of a paltry hundred or so. I tell you the colt is a dead certainty. If I could have got a thousand or two on him last week, we might have ended our dog days millionaires. Hand over what you can. You've money's worth, if not money. Where's that sapphire you stole?"

"I didn't. I can show you the receipted bill. All *I* possess is honestly come by. What could you do with it, even if I gave it you? You couldn't sell it as the Valdez, and you can't get it cut up as you might if it were real."

"If it's only bogus, why are you always in such a flutter about it? I'll do something with it, never fear. Hand over."

"I can't. I haven't got it. I had to raise something on it before I left town."

"Will you swear it's not in that wardrobe? I dare say you will. I mean to see. Give me those keys."

I heard a struggle and a jingle, then the wardrobe door must have been flung open, for a streak of light struck through a crack in the wood of the back. Creeping close and peeping through, I could see an awful sight. Lady Carwitchet in a flannel wrapper, minus hair, teeth, complexion, pointing a skinny forefinger that quivered with rage at her son, who was out of the range of my vision.

"Stop that, and throw those keys down here directly, or I'll rouse the house. Sir Thomas is a magistrate, and will lock you up as soon as look at you." She clutched at the bell rope as she spoke. "I'll swear I'm in danger of my life from you and give you in charge. Yes, and when you're in prison I'll keep you there till you die. I've often thought I'd do it. How about the hotel robberies last summer at Cowes, eh? Mightn't the police be grateful for a hint or two? And how about — "

The keys fell with a crash on the bed, accompanied by some bad language in an apologetic tone, and the door slammed to. I crept trembling to bed.

This new and horrible complication of the situation filled me with dismay. Lord Carwitchet's wolfish glance at my rubies took a new meaning. They were safe enough, I believed — but the sapphire! If he disbelieved his mother, how long would she be able to keep it from his clutches? That she had some plot of her own of which the bishop would eventually be the victim I did not doubt, or why had she not made her bargain with him long ago? But supposing she took fright, lost her head, allowed her son to wrest the jewel from her, or gave consent to its being mutilated, divided! I lay in a cold perspiration till morning.

My terrors haunted me all day. They were with me at breakfast time when Lady Carwitchet, tripping in smiling, made a last attempt to induce me to accompany her and keep her "bad, bad boy" from getting among "those horrid betting men."

They haunted me through the long peaceful day with Leta and the *tête-à-tête* dinner, but they swarmed around and beset me sorest when, sitting alone over my sitting-room fire, I listened for the return of the drag party. I read my newspaper and brewed myself some hot strong drink, but there comes a time of night when no fire can warm and no drink can cheer. The bishop's despairing face kept me company, and his troubles and the wrongs of the future heir took possession of me. Then the uncanny noises that make all old houses ghostly during the small hours began to make themselves heard. Muffled footsteps trod the corridor, stopping to listen at every door, door latches gently clicked, boards creaked unreasonably, sounds of stealthy movements came from the locked-up bathroom. The welcome crash of wheels at last, and the sound of the front-door bell. I could hear Lady Carwitchet making her shrill *adieux* to her friends and her steps in the corridor. She was softly humming a little song as she approached. I heard her unlock her bedroom door before she entered — an odd thing to do. Tom came sleepily stumbling to his room later. I put my head out. "Where is Lord Carwitchet?"

"Haven't you seen him? He left us hours ago. Not come home, eh? Well, he's welcome to stay away. I don't want to see more of him." Tom's brow was dark and his voice surly. "I gave him to understand as much." Whatever had happened, Tom was evidently too disgusted to explain just then.

I went back to my fire unaccountably relieved, and brewed myself another and a stronger brew. It warmed me this time, but excited me foolishly. There must be some way out of the difficulty. I felt now as if I could almost see it if I gave my mind to it. Why — suppose — there might be no difficulty after all! The bishop was a nervous old gentleman. He might have been mistaken all through, Bogaerts might have been mistaken, I might — no. I could not have been mistaken — or I thought not. I fidgeted and fumed and argued with myself till I found I should have no peace of mind without a look at the stone in my possession, and I actually went to the safe and took the case out.

The sapphire certainly looked different by lamplight. I sat and stared, and all but overpersuaded my better judgment into giving it a verdict. Bogaerts's mark — I suddenly remembered it. I took my magnifier and held the pendant to the light. There, scratched upon the stone, was the Greek Beta! There came a tap on my door, and before I could answer, the handle turned softly and Lord Carwitchet stood before me. I whipped the case into my dressing-gown pocket and stared at him. He was not pleasant to look at, especially at that time of night. He had a dishevelled, desperate air, his voice was hoarse, his red-rimmed eyes wild.

"I beg your pardon," he began civilly enough. "I

saw your light burning, and thought, as we go by the early train to-morrow, you might allow me to consult you now on a little business of my mother's." His eyes roved about the room. Was he trying to find the whereabouts of my safe? "You know a lot about precious stones, don't you?"

"So my friends are kind enough to say. Won't you sit down? I have unluckily little chance of indulging the taste on my own account," was my cautious reply.

"But you've written a book about them, and know them when you see them, don't you? Now my mother has given me something, and would like you to give a guess at its value. Perhaps you can put me in the way of disposing of it?"

"I certainly can do so if it is worth anything. Is that it?" I was in a fever of excitement, for I guessed what was clutched in his palm. He held out to me the Valdez sapphire.

How it shone and sparkled like a great blue star! I made myself a deprecating smile as I took it from him, but how dare I call it false to its face? As well accuse the sun in heaven of being a cheap imitation. I faltered and prevaricated feebly. Where was my moral courage, and where was the good, honest, thumping lie that should have aided me? "I have the best authority for recognizing this as a very good copy of a famous stone in the possession of the Bishop of Northchurch." His scowl grew so black that I saw he believed me, and I went on more cheerily: "This was manufactured by Johannes Bogaerts — I can give you his address, and you can make inquiries yourself — by special permission of the then owner, the late Leone Montanaro."

"Hand it back!" he interrupted (his other remarks were outrageous, but satisfactory to hear); but I waved him off. I couldn't give it up. It fascinated me. I toyed with it, I caressed it. I made it display its different tones of colour. I must see the two stones together. I must see it outshine its paltry rival. It was a whimsical frenzy that seized me — I can call it by no other name.

"Would you like to see the original? Curiously enough, I have it here. The bishop has left it in my charge."

The wolfish light flamed up in Carwitchet's eyes as I drew forth the case. He laid the Valdez down on a sheet of paper, and I placed the other, still in its case, beside it. In that moment they looked identical, except for the little loop of sham stones, replaced by a plain gold band in the bishop's jewel. Carwitchet leaned across the table eagerly, the table gave a lurch, the lamp tottered, crashed over, and we were left in semidarkness.

"Don't stir!" Carwitchet shouted. "The paraffin is all over the place!" He seized my sofa blanket, and flung it over the table while I stood helpless. "There, that's safe now. Have you candles on the chimneypiece? I've got matches."

He looked very white and excited as he lit up. "Might have been an awkward job with all that burning paraffin running about," he said quite pleasantly. "I hope no real harm is done." I was lifting the rug with shaking hands. The two stones lay as I had placed them. No! I nearly dropped it back again. It was the stone in the case that had the loop with the three sham sapphires!

Carwitchet picked the other up hastily. "So you

say this is rubbish?" he asked, his eyes sparkling wickedly, and an attempt at mortification in his tone.

"Utter rubbish!" I pronounced, with truth and decision, snapping up the case and pocketing it. "Lady Carwitchet must have known it."

"Ah, well, it's disappointing, isn't it? Good-by, we shall not meet again."

I shook hands with him most cordially. "Good-by, Lord Carwitchet. *So* glad to have met you and your mother. It has been a source of the *greatest* pleasure, I assure you."

I have never seen the Carwitchets since. The bishop drove over next day in rather better spirits. Miss Panton had refused the chaplain.

"It doesn't matter, my lord," I said to him heartily. "We've all been under some strange misconception. The stone in your possession is the veritable one. I could swear to that anywhere. The sapphire Lady Carwitchet wears is only an excellent imitation, and — I have seen it with my own eyes — is the one bearing Bogaerts's mark, the Greek Beta."

III. The Oblong Box — Edgar Allan Poe

Some years ago I engaged passage from Charleston, S. C., to the city of New York, in the fine packet-ship *Independence*, Captain Hardy. We were to sail on the fifteenth of the month (June), weather permitting; and on the fourteenth I went on board to arrange some matters in my stateroom.

I found that we were to have a great many passengers, including a more than usual number of ladies. On the list were several of my acquaintances; and among other names I was rejoiced to see that of Mr. Cornelius Wyatt, a young artist, for whom I entertained feelings of warm friendship. He had been, with me, a fellow-student at C— — University, where we were very much together. He had the ordinary temperament of genius, and was a compound of misanthropy, sensibility, and enthusiasm. To these qualities he united the warmest and truest heart which ever beat in a human bosom.

I observed that his name was carded upon three staterooms: and upon again referring to the list of passengers I found that he had engaged passage for himself, wife, and two sisters — his own. The staterooms were sufficiently roomy, and each had two berths, one above the other. These berths, to be sure, were so exceedingly narrow as to be insufficient for more than one person; still, I could not comprehend why there were three staterooms for these four persons. I was, just at that epoch, in one of those moody frames of mind which make a man abnormally inquisitive about trifles: and I confess with shame that I busied myself in a variety of ill-bred and preposterous conjectures about this matter of the supernumerary stateroom. It was no business of mine, to be sure; but with none the less pertinacity did I occupy myself in attempts to resolve the enigma. At last I reached a conclusion which wrought in me great wonder why I had not arrived at it before. "It is a servant, of course," I said; "what a fool I am not sooner to have thought of so obvious a solution!" And then I again repaired to the list, but here I saw distinctly that no servant was to come with the party: although, in fact, it had been the original design to bring one, for the words "and servant" had been first written and then overscored. "Oh, extra baggage, to be sure," I now said to myself; "something he wishes not to be put in the hold, something to be kept under his own eye, — ah, I have it! a painting or so, and this is what he has been bargaining about with Nicolino, the Italian Jew." This idea satisfied me and I dismissed my curiosity for the nonce.

Wyatt's two sisters I knew very well, and most amiable and clever girls they were. His wife he had newly married, and I had never yet seen her. He had often talked about her in my presence, however, and in his usual style of enthusiasm. He described her as of surpassing beauty, wit, and accomplishment. I was, therefore, quite anxious to make her acquaintance.

On the day in which I visited the ship (the fourteenth), Wyatt and party were also to visit it, so the Captain informed me, and I waited on board an hour longer than I had designed in hope of being presented to the bride; but then an apology came. "Mrs. W. was a little indisposed, and would decline coming on board until to-morrow at the hour of sailing."

The morrow having arrived, I was going from my hotel to the wharf, when Captain Hardy met me and said that, "owing to circumstances" (a stupid but convenient phrase), "he rather thought the *Independence* would not sail for a day or two, and that when all was ready he would send up and let me know." This I thought strange, for there was a stiff southerly breeze; but as "the circumstances" were not forthcoming, although I pumped for them with much perseverance, I had nothing to do but to return home and digest my impatience at leisure.

I did not receive the expected message from the Captain for nearly a week. It came at length, however, and I immediately went on board. The ship was crowded with passengers, and everything was in the bustle attendant upon making sail. Wyatt's party arrived in about ten minutes after myself. There were the two sisters, the bride, and the artist — the latter in one of his customary fits of moody misanthropy. I was too well used to these, however, to pay them any special attention. He did not even introduce me to his wife; this courtesy devolving, perforce, upon his sister Marian, a very sweet and intelligent girl, who in a few hurried words made us acquainted.

Mrs. Wyatt had been closely veiled; and when she raised her veil in acknowledging my bow, I confess that I was very profoundly astonished. I should have been much more so, however, had not long experience advised me not to trust, with too implicit a reliance, the enthusiastic descriptions of my friend the artist, when indulging in comments upon the loveliness of woman. When beauty was the theme, I well knew with what facility he soared into the regions of the purely ideal.

The truth is, I could not help regarding Mrs. Wyatt as a decidedly plain-looking woman. If not positively ugly, she was not, I think, very far from it. She was dressed, however, in exquisite taste, and then I had no doubt that she had captivated my friend's heart by the more enduring graces of the intellect and soul. She said very few words, and passed at once into her stateroom with Mr. W.

My old inquisitiveness now returned. There was no servant, that was a settled point. I looked, therefore, for the extra baggage. After some delay a cart arrived at the wharf with an oblong pine box, which was everything that seemed to be expected. Immediately upon its arrival we made sail, and in a short time were safely over the bar and standing out to sea.

The box in question was, as I say, oblong. It was about six feet in length by two and a half in breadth: I observed it attentively and like to be precise. Now, this shape was peculiar; and no sooner had I seen it than I took credit to myself for the accuracy of my guessing. I had reached the conclusion, it will be remembered, that the extra baggage of my friend the artist would prove to be pictures, or at least a picture, for I knew he had been for several weeks in conference with Nicolino; and now here was a box, which, from its shape, could possibly contain nothing in the world but a copy of Leonardo's *Last Supper*; and a copy of this very *Last Supper*, done by Rubini the younger at Florence, I had known for some time to be in the possession of Nicolino. This point, therefore, I considered as sufficiently settled. I chuckled excessively when I thought of my acumen. It was the first time I had ever known Wyatt to keep from me any of his artistical secrets; but here he evidently intended to steal a march upon me and smuggle a fine picture to New York, under my very nose; expecting me to know nothing of the matter. I resolved to quiz him well, now and hereafter.

One thing, however, annoyed me not a little. The box did not go into the extra stateroom. It was deposited in Wyatt's own; and there, too, it remained, occupying very nearly the whole of the floor, no doubt to the exceeding discomfort of the artist and his wife; this the more especially as the tar or paint with which it was lettered in sprawling capitals emitted a strong, disagreeable, and, to my fancy, a peculiarly disgusting odour. On the lid were painted the words: "Mrs. Adelaide Curtis, Albany, New York. Charge of Cornelius Wyatt, Esq. This side up. To be handled with care."

Now, I was aware that Mrs. Adelaide Curtis of Albany was the artist's wife's mother; but then I looked upon the whole address as a mystification, intended especially for myself. I made up my mind, of course, that the box and contents would never get farther north than the studio of my misanthropic friend in Chambers Street, New York.

For the first three or four days we had fine weather, although the wind was dead ahead, having chopped round to the northward immediately upon our losing sight of the coast. The passengers were, consequently, in high spirits and disposed to be social. I must except, however, Wyatt and his sisters, who behaved stiffly, and, I could not help thinking, uncourteously, to the rest of the party. Wyatt's conduct I did not so much regard. He was gloomy, even beyond his usual habit, — in fact, he was morose; but in him I was prepared for eccentricity. For the sisters, however, I could make no excuse. They secluded themselves in their staterooms during the greater part of the passage, and absolutely refused, although I repeatedly urged them, to hold communication with any person on board.

Mrs. Wyatt herself was far more agreeable. That is to say, she was chatty; and to be chatty is no slight recommendation at sea. She became excessively intimate with most of the ladies; and, to my profound astonishment, evinced no equivocal disposition to coquet with the men. She amused us all very much. I say "amused," and scarcely know how to explain myself. The truth is, I soon found that Mrs. W. was far oftener laughed at than with. The gentlemen said little about her; but the ladies in a little while pronounced her "a good-hearted thing, rather indifferent-looking, totally uneducated, and decidedly vulgar." The great wonder was, how Wyatt had been entrapped into such a match. Wealth was the general solution, but this I knew to be no solution at all; for Wyatt had told me that she neither brought him a dollar nor had any expectations from any source whatever. "He had married," he said, "for love, and for love only; and his bride was far more than worthy of his love." When I thought of these expressions on the part of my friend, I confess that I felt indescribably puzzled. Could it be possible that he was taking leave of his senses? What else could I think? He, so refined, so intellectual, so fastidious, with so exquisite a perception of the faulty, and so keen an appreciation of the beautiful! To be sure, the lady seemed especially fond of him, particularly so in his absence, when she made herself ridiculous by frequent quotations of what had been said by her "beloved husband, Mr. Wyatt." The word "husband" seemed forever, to use one of her own delicate expressions, — forever "on the tip of her tongue." In the meantime it was observed by all on board that he avoided her in the most pointed manner, and, for the most part, shut himself up alone in his stateroom, where, in fact, he might have been said to live altogether, leaving his wife at full liberty to amuse herself as she thought best in the public society of the main cabin.

My conclusion, from what I saw and heard, was that the artist, by some unaccountable freak of fate, or perhaps in some fit of enthusiastic and fanciful passion, had been induced to unite himself with a person altogether beneath him, and that the natural result, entire and speedy disgust, had ensued. I pitied him from the bottom of my heart, but could not, for that reason, quite forgive his incommunicativeness in the matter of the *Last Supper*. For this I resolved to have my revenge.

One day he came up on deck, and, taking his arm as had been my wont, I sauntered with him backward and forward. His gloom, however (which I considered quite natural under the circumstances), seemed entirely unabated. He said little, and that moodily, and with evident effort. I ventured a jest or two, and he made a sickening attempt at a smile. Poor fellow! as I thought of his wife I wondered that he could have heart to put on even the semblance of mirth. At last I ventured a home thrust. I determined to commence a series of covert insinuations, or innuendos, about the oblong box, just to let him perceive, gradually, that I was not altogether the butt, or victim, of his little bit of pleasant mystification. My first observation was by way of opening a masked battery. I said something about the "peculiar shape of that box"; and, as I spoke the words I smiled knowingly, winked, and touched him gently with my forefinger in the ribs.

The manner in which Wyatt received this harmless pleasantry convinced me at once that he was mad. At first he stared at me as if he found it impossible to comprehend the witticism of my remark; but as its point seemed slowly to make its way into his brain, his eyes, in the same proportion, seemed protruding from their sockets. Then he grew very red, then hideously pale, then, as if highly amused with what I had insinuated, he began a loud and boisterous laugh, which, to my astonishment, he kept up, with gradually increasing vigour, for ten minutes or more. In conclusion, he fell flat and heavily upon the deck. When I ran to uplift him, to all appearance he was dead.

I called assistance, and, with much difficulty, we brought him to himself. Upon reviving he spoke incoherently for some time. At length we bled him and put him to bed. The next morning he was quite recovered, so far as regarded his mere bodily health. Of his mind I say nothing, of course. I avoided him during the rest of the passage, by advice of the Captain, who seemed to coincide with me altogether in my views of his insanity, but cautioned me to say nothing on this head to any person on board.

Several circumstances occurred immediately after this fit of Wyatt's which contributed to heighten the curiosity with which I was already possessed. Among other things, this: I had been nervous; drank too much strong green tea, and slept ill at night, — in fact, for two nights I could not be properly said to sleep at all. Now, my stateroom opened into the main cabin or dining-room, as did those of all the single men on board. Wyatt's three rooms were in the after-cabin, which was separated from the main one by a slight sliding door, never locked even at night. As we were almost constantly on a wind, and the breeze was not a little stiff, the ship heeled to leeward very considerably; and whenever her starboard side was to leeward the sliding door between the cabins slid open and so remained, nobody taking the trouble to get up and shut it. But my berth was in such a position that when my own stateroom door was open, as well as the sliding door in question (and my own door was always open on account of the heat), I could see into the after-cabin quite distinctly, and just at that portion of it, too, where were situated the staterooms of Mr. Wyatt. Well, during two nights (not consecutive), while I lay awake, I clearly saw Mrs. W., about eleven o'clock upon each night, steal cautiously from the stateroom of Mr. W. and enter the extra room, where she remained until daybreak, when she was called by her husband and went back. That they were virtually separated was clear. They had separate apartments, no doubt in contemplation of a more permanent divorce; and here, after all, I thought, was the mystery of the extra stateroom.

There was another circumstance, too, which interested me much. During the two wakeful nights in question, and immediately after the disappearance of Mrs. Wyatt into the extra stateroom, I was attracted by certain singular, cautious, subdued noises in that of her husband. After listening to them for some time with thoughtful attention, I at length succeeded perfectly in translating their import. They were sounds occasioned by the artist in prying open the oblong box by means of a chisel and mallet, the latter being apparently muffled or deadened by some soft woollen or cotton substance in which its head was enveloped.

In this manner I fancied I could distinguish the precise moment when he fairly disengaged the lid, also that I could determine when he removed it altogether, and when he deposited it upon the lower berth in his room; this latter point I knew, for example, by certain slight taps which the lid made in striking against the wooden edges of the berth as he endeavoured to lay it down very gently, there being no room for it on the floor. After this there was a dead stillness, and I heard nothing more, upon either occasion, until nearly daybreak; unless, perhaps, I may mention a low sobbing or murmuring sound, so very much suppressed as to be nearly inaudible, if, indeed, the whole of this latter noise were not rather produced by my own imagination. I say it seemed to resemble sobbing or sighing, but, of course, it could not have been either. I rather think it was a ringing in my own ears. Mr. Wyatt, no doubt, according to custom, was merely giving the rein to one of his hobbies, indulging in one of his fits of artistic enthusiasm. He had opened his oblong box in order to feast his eyes on the pictorial treasure within. There was nothing in this, however, to make him sob. I repeat, therefore, that it must have been simply a freak of my own fancy, distempered by good Captain Hardy's green tea. Just before dawn, on each of the two nights of which I speak, I distinctly heard Mr. Wyatt replace the lid upon the oblong box, and force the nails into their old places by means of the muffled mallet. Having done this, he issued from his stateroom, fully dressed, and proceeded to call Mrs. W. from hers.

We had been at sea seven days, and were now off Cape Hatteras, when there came a tremendously heavy blow from the southwest. We were, in a measure, prepared for it, however, as the weather had been holding out threats for some time. Everything was made snug, alow and aloft; and, as the wind steadily freshened, we lay to, at length, under spanker and foretopsail, both double-reefed.

In this trim we rode safely enough for forty-eight hours, the ship proving herself an excellent sea-boat in many respects, and shipping no water of any consequence. At the end of this period, however, the gale had freshened into a hurricane, and our after-sail split into ribbons, bringing us so much in the trough of the water that we shipped several prodigious seas, one immediately after the other. By this accident we lost three men overboard with the caboose, and nearly the whole of the larboard bulwarks. Scarcely had we recovered our senses before the foretopsail went into shreds, when we got up a storm staysail, and with this did pretty well for some hours, the ship heading the sea much more steadily than before.

The gale still held on, however, and we saw no signs of its abating. The rigging was found to be ill-fitted and greatly strained; and on the third day of the blow, about five in the afternoon, our mizzen-mast, in a heavy lurch to windward, went by the board. For an hour or more we tried in vain to get rid of it, on account of the prodigious rolling of the ship; and, before we had succeeded, the carpenter came aft and announced four feet water in the hold. To add to our dilemma, we found the pumps choked and nearly useless.

All was now confusion and despair, but an effort was made to lighten the ship by throwing overboard as much of her cargo as could be reached, and by cutting away the two masts that remained. This we at last accomplished, but we were still unable to do anything at the pumps; and, in the meantime, the leak gained on us very fast.

At sundown the gale had sensibly diminished in violence, and, as the sea went down with it, we still entertained faint hopes of saving ourselves in the boats. At eight P.M., the clouds broke away to windward, and we had the advantage of a full moon, a piece of good fortune which served wonderfully to cheer our drooping spirits.

After incredible labour we succeeded, at length, in getting the long-boat over the side without material accident, and into this we crowded the whole of the crew and most of the passengers. This party made off immediately, and, after undergoing much suffering, finally arrived in safety at Ocracoke Inlet, on the third day after the wreck.

Fourteen passengers, with the Captain, remained on board, resolving to trust their fortunes to the jolly-boat at the stern. We lowered it without difficulty, although it was only by a miracle that we prevented it from swamping as it touched the water. It contained, when afloat, the Captain and his wife, Mr. Wyatt and party, a Mexican officer, wife, four children, and myself, with a negro valet.

We had no room, of course, for anything except a few positively necessary instruments, some provisions, and the clothes upon our backs. No one had thought of even attempting to save anything more. What must have been the astonishment of all, then, when, having proceeded a few fathoms from the ship, Mr. Wyatt stood up in the stern-sheets and coolly demanded of Captain Hardy that the boat should be put back for the purpose of taking in his oblong box!

"Sit down, Mr. Wyatt," replied the Captain, somewhat sternly; "you will capsize us if you do not sit quite still. Our gunwale is almost in the water now."

"The box!" vociferated Mr. Wyatt, still standing, "the box, I say! Captain Hardy, you cannot, you will not refuse me. Its weight will be but a trifle, it is nothing, mere nothing. By the mother who bore you — for the love of Heaven — by your hope of salvation, I implore you to put back for the box!"

The Captain for a moment seemed touched by the earnest appeal of the artist, but he regained his stern composure, and merely said:

"Mr. Wyatt, you are mad. I cannot listen to you. Sit down, I say, or you will swamp the boat. Stay! hold him, seize him! he is about to spring overboard! There — I knew it — he is over!"

As the Captain said this, Mr. Wyatt, in fact, sprang from the boat, and, as we were yet in the lee of the wreck, succeeded, by almost superhuman exertion, in getting hold of a rope which hung from the forechains. In another moment he was on board, and rushing frantically down into the cabin.

In the meantime we had been swept astern of the ship, and being quite out of her lee, were at the mercy of the tremendous sea which was still running. We made a determined effort to put back, but our little boat was like a feather in the breath of the tempest. We saw at a glance that the doom of the unfortunate artist was sealed.

As our distance from the wreck rapidly increased, the madman (for as such only could we regard him) was seen to emerge from the companionway, up which, by dint of strength that appeared gigantic, he dragged, bodily, the oblong box. While we gazed in the extremity of astonishment, he passed rapidly several turns of a three-inch rope, first around the box and then around his body. In another instant both body and box were in the sea, disappearing suddenly, at once and forever.

We lingered awhile sadly upon our oars, with our eyes riveted upon the spot. At length we pulled away. The silence remained unbroken for an hour. Finally I hazarded a remark.

"Did you observe, Captain, how suddenly they sank? Was not that an exceedingly singular thing? I confess that I entertained some feeble hope of his final deliverance when I saw him lash himself to the box and commit himself to the sea."

"They sank as a matter of course," replied the Captain, "and that like a shot. They will soon rise again, however, but not till the salt melts."

"The salt!" I ejaculated.

"Hush!" said the Captain, pointing to the wife and sisters of the deceased. "We must talk of these things at some more appropriate time."

*****

We suffered much and made a narrow escape; but fortune befriended us, as well as our mates in the long-boat. We landed, in fine, more dead than alive, after four days of intense distress, upon the beach opposite Roanoke Island. We remained here a week, were not ill-treated by the wreckers, and at length obtained a passage to New York.

About a month after the loss of the *Independence*, I happened to meet Captain Hardy in Broadway. Our conversation turned, naturally, upon the disaster, and especially upon the sad fate of poor Wyatt. I thus learned the following particulars:

The artist had engaged passage for himself, wife, two sisters, and a servant. His wife was indeed, as she had been represented, a most lovely and most accomplished woman. On the morning of the fourteenth of June (the day in which I first visited the ship), the lady suddenly sickened and died. The young husband was frantic with grief, but circumstances imperatively forbade the deferring his voyage to New York. It was necessary to take to her mother the corpse of his adored wife, and, on the other hand, the universal prejudice which would prevent his doing so openly was well known. Nine tenths of the passengers would have abandoned the ship rather than take passage with a dead body.

In this dilemma Captain Hardy arranged that the corpse, being first partially embalmed and packed, with a large quantity of salt in a box of suitable dimensions, should be conveyed on board as merchandise. Nothing was to be said of the lady's decease; and, as it was well understood that Mr. Wyatt had engaged passage for his wife, it became necessary that some person should personate her during the voyage. This the deceased lady's maid was easily prevailed on to do. The extra stateroom, originally engaged for this girl during her mistress's life, was now merely retained. In this stateroom the pseudo-wife slept, of course, every night. In the daytime she performed, to the best of her ability, the part of her mistress, whose person, it had been carefully ascertained, was unknown to any of the passengers on board.

My own mistake arose, naturally enough, through too careless, too inquisitive, and too impulsive a temperament. But of late it is a rare thing that I sleep soundly at night. There is a countenance which haunts me, turn as I will. There is an hysterical laugh which will forever ring within my ears.

IV. The Birth-Mark — Nathaniel Hawthorne

In the latter part of the last century, there lived a man of science — an eminent proficient in every branch of natural philosophy — who, not long before our story opens, had made experience of a spiritual affinity, more attractive than any chemical one. He had left his laboratory to the care of an assistant, cleared his fine countenance from the furnace-smoke, washed the stain of acids from his fingers, and persuaded a beautiful woman to become his wife. In those days, when the comparatively recent discovery of electricity, and other kindred mysteries of nature, seemed to open paths into the region of miracle, it was not unusual for the love of science to rival the love of woman, in its depth and absorbing energy. The higher intellect, the imagination, the spirit, and even the heart, might all find their congenial aliment in pursuits which, as some of their ardent votaries believed, would ascend from one step of powerful intelligence to another, until the philosopher should lay his hand on the secret of creative force, and perhaps make new worlds for himself. We know not whether Aylmer possessed this degree of faith in man's ultimate control over nature. He had devoted himself, however, too unreservedly to scientific studies, ever to be weaned from them by any second passion. His love for his young wife might prove the stronger of the two; but it could only be by intertwining itself with his love of science, and uniting the strength of the latter to its own.

Such an union accordingly took place, and was attended with truly remarkable consequences, and a deeply impressive moral. One day, very soon after their marriage, Aylmer sat gazing at his wife, with a trouble in his countenance that grew stronger, until he spoke.

"Georgiana," said he, "has it never occurred to you that the mark upon your cheek might be removed?"

"No, indeed," said she, smiling; but perceiving the seriousness of his manner, she blushed deeply. "To tell you the truth, it has been so often called a charm, that I was simple enough to imagine it might be so."

"Ah, upon another face, perhaps it might," replied her husband. "But never on yours! No, dearest Georgiana, you came so nearly perfect from the hand of Nature, that this slightest possible defect — which we hesitate whether to term a defect or a beauty — shocks me, as being the visible mark of earthly imperfection."

"Shocks you, my husband!" cried Georgiana, deeply hurt; at first reddening with momentary anger, but then bursting into tears. "Then why did you take me from my mother's side? You cannot love what shocks you!"

To explain this conversation, it must be mentioned, that, in the centre of Georgiana's left cheek, there was a singular mark, deeply interwoven, as it were, with the texture and substance of her face. In the usual state of her complexion, — a healthy, though delicate bloom, — the mark wore a tint of deeper crimson, which imperfectly defined its shape amid the surrounding rosiness. When she blushed, it gradually became more indistinct, and finally vanished amid the triumphant rush of blood, that bathed the whole cheek with its brilliant glow. But, if any shifting emotion caused her to turn pale, there was the mark again, a crimson stain upon the snow, in what Aylmer sometimes deemed an almost fearful distinctness. Its shape bore not a little similarity to the human hand, though of the smallest pigmy size. Georgiana's lovers were wont to say, that some fairy, at her birth-hour, had laid her tiny hand upon the infant's cheek, and left this impress there, in token of the magic endowments that were to give her such sway over all hearts. Many a desperate swain would have risked life for the privilege of pressing his lips to the mysterious hand. It must not be concealed, however, that the impression wrought by this fairy sign-manual varied exceedingly, according to the difference of temperament in the beholders. Some fastidious persons — but they were exclusively of her own sex — affirmed that the Bloody Hand, as they chose to call it, quite destroyed the effect of Georgiana's beauty, and rendered her countenance even hideous. But it would be as reasonable to say, that one of those small blue stains, which sometimes occur in the purest statuary marble, would convert the Eve of Powers to a monster. Masculine observers, if the birth-mark did not heighten their admiration, contented themselves with wishing it away, that the world might possess one living specimen of ideal loveliness, without the semblance of a flaw. After his marriage — for he thought little or nothing of the matter before — Aylmer discovered that this was the case with himself.

Had she been less beautiful — if Envy's self could have found aught else to sneer at — he might have felt his affection heightened by the prettiness of this mimic hand, now vaguely portrayed, now lost, now stealing forth again, and glimmering to-and-fro with every pulse of emotion that throbbed within her heart. But, seeing her otherwise so perfect, he found this one defect grow more and more intolerable, with every moment of their united lives. It was the fatal flaw of humanity, which Nature, in one shape or another, stamps ineffaceably on all her productions, either to imply that they are temporary and finite, or that their perfection must be wrought by toil and pain. The Crimson Hand expressed the ineludible gripe, in which mortality clutches the highest and purest of earthly mould, degrading them into kindred with the lowest, and even with the very brutes, like whom their visible frames return to dust. In this manner, selecting it as the symbol of his wife's liability to sin, sorrow, decay, and death, Aylmer's sombre imagination was not long in rendering the birth-mark a frightful object, causing him more trouble and horror than ever Georgiana's beauty, whether of soul or sense, had given him delight.

At all the seasons which should have been their happiest, he invariably, and without intending it — nay, in spite of a purpose to the contrary — reverted to this one disastrous topic. Trifling as it at first appeared, it so connected itself with innumerable trains of thought, and modes of feeling, that it became the central point of all. With the morning twilight, Aylmer opened his eyes upon his wife's face, and recognized the symbol of imperfection; and when they sat together at the evening hearth, his eyes wandered stealthily to her cheek, and beheld, flickering with the blaze of the wood fire, the spectral Hand that wrote mortality where he would fain have worshipped. Georgiana soon learned to shudder at his gaze. It needed but a glance, with the peculiar expression that his face often wore, to change the roses of her cheek into a death-like paleness, amid which the Crimson Hand was brought strongly out, like a bas-relief of ruby on the whitest marble.

Late, one night, when the lights were growing dim, so as hardly to betray the stain on the poor wife's cheek, she herself, for the first time, voluntarily took up the subject.

"Do you remember, my dear Aylmer," said she, with a feeble attempt at a smile — "have you any recollection of a dream, last night, about this odious Hand?"

"None! — none whatever!" replied Aylmer, starting; but then he added in a dry, cold tone, affected for the sake of concealing the real depth of his emotion: — "I might well dream of it; for, before I fell asleep, it had taken a pretty firm hold of my fancy."

"And you did dream of it," continued Georgiana hastily; for she dreaded lest a gush of tears should interrupt what she had to say — "A terrible dream! I wonder that you can forget it. Is it possible to forget this one expression? — 'It is in her heart now — we must have it out!' — Reflect, my husband; for by all means I would have you recall that dream."

The mind is in a sad state, when Sleep, the all-involving, cannot confine her spectres within the dim region of her sway, but suffers them to break forth, affrighting this actual life with secrets that perchance belong to a deeper one. Aylmer now remembered his dream. He had fancied himself, with his servant Aminadab, attempting an operation for the removal of the birth-mark. But the deeper went the knife, the deeper sank the Hand, until at length its tiny grasp appeared to have caught hold of Georgiana's heart; whence, however, her husband was inexorably resolved to cut or wrench it away.

When the dream had shaped itself perfectly in his memory, Aylmer sat in his wife's presence with a guilty feeling. Truth often finds its way to the mind close-muffled in robes of sleep, and then speaks with uncompromising directness of matters in regard to which we practise an unconscious self-deception, during our waking moments. Until now, he had not been aware of the tyrannizing influence acquired by one idea over his mind, and of the lengths which he might find in his heart to go, for the sake of giving himself peace.

"Aylmer," resumed Georgiana, solemnly, "I know not what may be the cost to both of us, to rid me of this fatal birth-mark. Perhaps its removal may cause cureless deformity. Or, it may be, the stain goes as deep as life itself. Again, do we know that there is a possibility, on any terms, of unclasping the firm gripe of this little Hand, which was laid upon me before I came into the world?"

"Dearest Georgiana, I have spent much thought upon the subject," hastily interrupted Aylmer — "I am convinced of the perfect practicability of its removal."

"If there be the remotest possibility of it," continued Georgiana, "let the attempt be made, at whatever risk. Danger is nothing to me; for life — while this hateful mark makes me the object of your horror and disgust — life is a burthen which I would fling down with joy. Either remove this dreadful Hand, or take my wretched life! You have deep science! All the world bears witness of it. You have achieved great wonders! Cannot you remove this little, little mark, which I cover with the tips of two small fingers! Is this beyond your power, for the sake of your own peace, and to save your poor wife from madness?"

"Noblest — dearest — tenderest wife!" cried Aylmer, rapturously. "Doubt not my power. I have already given this matter the deepest thought — thought which might almost have enlightened me to create a being less perfect than yourself. Georgiana, you have led me deeper than ever into the heart of science. I feel myself fully competent to render this dear cheek as faultless as its fellow; and then, most beloved, what will be my triumph, when I shall have corrected what Nature left imperfect, in her fairest work! Even Pygmalion, when his sculptured woman assumed life, felt not greater ecstasy than mine will be."

"It is resolved, then," said Georgiana, faintly smiling, — "And, Aylmer, spare me not, though you should find the birth-mark take refuge in my heart at last."

Her husband tenderly kissed her cheek — her right cheek — not that which bore the impress of the Crimson Hand.

The next day, Aylmer apprised his wife of a plan that he had formed, whereby he might have opportunity for the intense thought and constant watchfulness which the proposed operation would require; while Georgiana, likewise, would enjoy the perfect repose essential to its success. They were to seclude themselves in the extensive apartments occupied by Aylmer as a laboratory, and where, during his toilsome youth, he had made discoveries in the elemental powers of nature, that had roused the admiration of all the learned societies in Europe.

Seated calmly in this laboratory, the pale philosopher had investigated the secrets of the highest cloud-region, and of the profoundest mines; he had satisfied himself of the causes that kindled and kept alive the fires of the volcano; and had explained the mystery of fountains, and how it is that they gush forth, some so bright and pure, and others with such rich medicinal virtues, from the dark bosom of the earth. Here, too, at an earlier period, he had studied the wonders of the human frame, and attempted to fathom the very process by which Nature assimilates all her precious influences from earth and air, and from the spiritual world, to create and foster Man, her masterpiece. The latter pursuit, however, Aylmer had long laid aside, in unwilling recognition of the truth, against which all seekers sooner or later stumble, that our great creative Mother, while she amuses us with apparently working in the broadest sunshine, is yet severely careful to keep her own secrets, and, in spite of her pretended openness, shows us nothing but results. She permits us indeed to mar, but seldom to mend, and, like a jealous patentee, on no account to make. Now, however, Aylmer resumed these half-forgotten investigations; not, of course, with such hopes or wishes as first suggested them; but because they involved much physiological truth, and lay in the path of his proposed scheme for the treatment of Georgiana.

As he led her over the threshold of the laboratory, Georgiana was cold and tremulous. Aylmer looked cheerfully into her face, with intent to reassure her, but was so startled with the intense glow of the birth-mark upon the whiteness of her cheek, that he could not restrain a strong convulsive shudder. His wife fainted.

"Aminadab! Aminadab!" shouted Aylmer,

stamping violently on the floor.

Forthwith, there issued from an inner apartment a man of low stature, but bulky frame, with shaggy hair hanging about his visage, which was grimed with the vapours of the furnace. This personage had been Aylmer's under-worker during his whole scientific career, and was admirably fitted for that office by his great mechanical readiness, and the skill with which, while incapable of comprehending a single principle, he executed all the practical details of his master's experiments. With his vast strength, his shaggy hair, his smoky aspect, and the indescribable earthiness that encrusted him, he seemed to represent man's physical nature; while Aylmer's slender figure, and pale, intellectual face, were no less apt a type of the spiritual element.

"Throw open the door of the boudoir, Aminadab," said Aylmer, "and burn a pastille."

"Yes, master," answered Aminadab, looking intently at the lifeless form of Georgiana; and then he muttered to himself: — "If she were my wife, I'd never part with that birth-mark."

When Georgiana recovered consciousness, she found herself breathing an atmosphere of penetrating fragrance, the gentle potency of which had recalled her from her death-like faintness. The scene around her looked like enchantment. Aylmer had converted those smoky, dingy, sombre rooms, where he had spent his brightest years in recondite pursuits, into a series of beautiful apartments, not unfit to be the secluded abode of a lovely woman. The walls were hung with gorgeous curtains, which imparted the combination of grandeur and grace, that no other species of adornment can achieve; and as they fell from the ceiling to the floor, their rich and ponderous folds, concealing all angles and straight lines, appeared to shut in the scene from infinite space. For aught Georgiana knew, it might be a pavilion among the clouds. And Aylmer, excluding the sunshine, which would have interfered with his chemical processes, had supplied its place with perfumed lamps, emitting flames of various hue, but all uniting in a soft, empurpled radiance. He now knelt by his wife's side, watching her earnestly, but without alarm; for he was confident in his science, and felt that he could draw a magic circle round her, within which no evil might intrude.

"Where am I? — Ah, I remember!" said Georgiana, faintly; and she placed her hand over her cheek, to hide the terrible mark from her husband's eyes.

"Fear not, dearest!" exclaimed he. "Do not shrink from me! Believe me, Georgiana, I even rejoice in this single imperfection, since it will be such a rapture to remove it."

"Oh, spare me!" sadly replied his wife. "Pray do not look at it again. I never can forget that convulsive shudder."

In order to soothe Georgiana, and, as it were, to release her mind from the burthen of actual things, Aylmer now put in practice some of the light and playful secrets which science had taught him among its profounder lore. Airy figures, absolutely bodiless ideas, and forms of unsubstantial beauty, came and danced before her, imprinting their momentary footsteps on beams of light. Though she had some indistinct idea of the method of these optical phenomena, still the illusion was almost perfect enough to warrant the belief that her husband possessed sway over the spiritual world. Then again, when she felt a wish to look forth from her seclusion, immediately, as if her thoughts were answered, the procession of external existence flitted across a screen. The scenery and the figures of actual life were perfectly represented, but with that bewitching, yet indescribable difference, which always makes a picture, an image, or a shadow, so much more attractive than the original. When wearied of this, Aylmer bade her cast her eyes upon a vessel, containing a quantity of earth. She did so, with little interest at first, but was soon startled, to perceive the germ of a plant, shooting upward from the soil. Then came the slender stalk — the leaves gradually unfolded themselves — and amid them was a perfect and lovely flower.

"It is magical!" cried Georgiana, "I dare not touch it."

"Nay, pluck it," answered Aylmer, "pluck it, and inhale its brief perfume while you may. The flower will wither in a few moments, and leave nothing save its brown seed-vessels — but thence may be perpetuated a race as ephemeral as itself."

But Georgiana had no sooner touched the flower than the whole plant suffered a blight, its leaves turning coal-black, as if by the agency of fire.

"There was too powerful a stimulus," said Aylmer thoughtfully.

To make up for this abortive experiment, he proposed to take her portrait by a scientific process of his own invention. It was to be effected by rays of light striking upon a polished plate of metal. Georgiana assented — but, on looking at the result, was affrighted to find the features of the portrait blurred and indefinable; while the minute figure of a hand appeared where the cheek should have been. Aylmer snatched the metallic plate, and threw it into a jar of corrosive acid.

Soon, however, he forgot these mortifying failures. In the intervals of study and chemical experiment, he came to her, flushed and exhausted, but seemed invigorated by her presence, and spoke in glowing language of the resources of his art. He gave a history of the long dynasty of the Alchemists, who spent so many ages in quest of the universal solvent, by which the Golden Principle might be elicited from all things vile and base. Aylmer appeared to believe, that, by the plainest scientific logic, it was altogether within the limits of possibility to discover this long-sought medium; but, he added, a philosopher who should go deep enough to acquire the power, would attain too lofty a wisdom to stoop to the exercise of it. Not less singular were his opinions in regard to the Elixir Vitæ. He more than intimated, that it was at his option to concoct a liquid that should prolong life for years — perhaps interminably — but that it would produce a discord in nature, which all the world, and chiefly the quaffer of the immortal nostrum, would find cause to curse.

"Aylmer, are you in earnest?" asked Georgiana, looking at him with amazement and fear; "it is terrible to possess such power, or even to dream of possessing it!"

"Oh, do not tremble, my love!" said her husband, "I would not wrong either you or myself, by working such inharmonious effects upon our lives. But I would have you consider how trifling, in comparison, is the skill requisite to remove this little Hand."

At the mention of the birth-mark, Georgiana, as usual, shrank, as if a red-hot iron had touched her cheek.

Again Aylmer applied himself to his labours. She could hear his voice in the distant furnace-room, giving directions to Aminadab, whose harsh, uncouth, misshapen tones were audible in response, more like the grunt or growl of a brute than human speech. After hours of absence, Aylmer reappeared, and proposed that she should now examine his cabinet of chemical products, and natural treasures of the earth. Among the former he showed her a small vial, in which, he remarked, was contained a gentle yet most powerful fragrance, capable of impregnating all the breezes that blow across a kingdom. They were of inestimable value, the contents of that little vial; and, as he said so, he threw some of the perfume into the air, and filled the room with piercing and invigorating delight.

"And what is this?" asked Georgiana, pointing to a small crystal globe, containing a gold-coloured liquid. "It is so beautiful to the eye, that I could imagine it the Elixir of Life."

"In one sense it is," replied Aylmer, "or rather the Elixir of Immortality. It is the most precious poison that ever was concocted in this world. By its aid, I could apportion the life-time of any mortal at whom you might point your finger. The strength of the dose would determine whether he were to linger out years, or drop dead in the midst of a breath. No king, on his guarded throne, could keep his life, if I, in my private station, should deem that the welfare of millions justified me in depriving him of it."

"Why do you keep such a terrible drug?" inquired Georgiana in horror.

"Do not mistrust me, dearest!" said her husband, smiling; "its virtuous potency is yet greater than its harmful one. But, see! here is a powerful cosmetic. With a few drops of this, in a vase of water, freckles may be washed away as easily as the hands are cleansed. A stronger infusion would take the blood out of the cheek, and leave the rosiest beauty a pale ghost."

"Is it with this lotion that you intend to bathe my cheek?" asked Georgiana, anxiously.

"Oh, no!" hastily replied her husband, — "this is merely superficial. Your case demands a remedy that shall go deeper."

In his interviews with Georgiana, Aylmer generally made minute inquiries as to her sensations, and whether the confinement of the rooms, and the temperature of the atmosphere, agreed with her. These questions had such a particular drift, that Georgiana began to conjecture that she was already subjected to certain physical influences, either breathed in with the fragrant air, or taken with her food. She fancied, likewise — but it might be altogether fancy — that there was a stirring up of her system: a strange, indefinite sensation creeping through her veins, and tingling, half-painfully, half-pleasurably, at her heart. Still, whenever she dared to look into the mirror, there she beheld herself, pale as a white rose, and with the crimson birth-mark stamped upon her cheek. Not even Aylmer now hated it so much as she.

To dispel the tedium of the hours which her husband found it necessary to devote to the processes of combination and analysis, Georgiana turned over the volumes of his scientific library. In many dark old tomes, she met with chapters full of romance and poetry. They were the works of the philosophers of the middle ages, such as Albertus, Magnus, Cornelius Agrippa, Paracelsus, and the famous friar who created the prophetic Brazen Head. All these antique naturalists stood in advance of their centuries, yet were imbued with some of their credulity, and therefore were believed, and perhaps imagined themselves, to have acquired from the investigation of nature a power above nature, and from physics a sway over the spiritual world. Hardly less curious and imaginative were the early volumes of the Transactions of the Royal Society, in which the members, knowing little of the limits of natural possibility, were continually recording wonders, or proposing methods whereby wonders might be wrought.

But, to Georgiana, the most engrossing volume was a large folio from her husband's own hand, in which he had recorded every experiment of his scientific career, with its original aim, the methods adopted for its development, and its final success or failure, with the circumstances to which either event was attributable. The book, in truth, was both the history and emblem of his ardent, ambitious, imaginative, yet practical and laborious, life. He handled physical details, as if there were nothing beyond them; yet spiritualized them all, and redeemed himself from materialism, by his strong and eager aspiration towards the infinite. In his grasp, the veriest clod of earth assumed a soul. Georgiana, as she read, reverenced Aylmer, and loved him more profoundly than ever, but with a less entire dependence on his judgment than heretofore. Much as he had accomplished, she could not but observe that his most splendid successes were almost invariably failures, if compared with the ideal at which he aimed. His brightest diamonds were the merest pebbles, and felt to be so by himself, in comparison with the inestimable gems which lay hidden beyond his reach. The volume, rich with achievements that had won renown for its author, was yet as melancholy a record as ever mortal hand had penned. It was the sad confession, and continual exemplification, of the short-comings of the composite man — the spirit burthened with clay and working in matter; and of the despair that assails the higher nature, at finding itself so miserably thwarted by the earthly part. Perhaps every man of genius, in whatever sphere, might recognize the image of his own experience in Aylmer's journal.

So deeply did these reflections affect Georgiana, that she laid her face upon the open volume, and burst into tears. In this situation she was found by her husband.

"It is dangerous to read in a sorcerer's books," said he, with a smile, though his countenance was uneasy and displeased. "Georgiana, there are pages in that volume, which I can scarcely glance over and keep my senses. Take heed lest it prove as detrimental to you!"

"It has made me worship you more than ever," said she.

"Ah! wait for this one success," rejoined he, "then worship me if you will. I shall deem myself hardly unworthy of it. But, come! I have sought you for the luxury of your voice. Sing to me, dearest!"

So she poured out the liquid music of her voice to quench the thirst of his spirit. He then took his leave, with a boyish exuberance of gaiety, assuring her that her seclusion would endure but a little longer, and that the result was already certain. Scarcely had he departed, when Georgiana felt irresistibly impelled to follow him. She had forgotten to inform Aylmer of a symptom, which, for two or three hours past, had begun to excite her attention. It was a sensation in the fatal birth-mark, not painful, but which induced a restlessness throughout her system. Hastening after her husband, she intruded, for the first time, into the laboratory.

The first thing that struck her eyes was the furnace, that hot and feverish worker, with the intense glow of its fire, which, by the quantities of soot clustered above it, seemed to have been burning for ages. There was a distilling apparatus in full operation. Around the room were retorts, tubes, cylinders, crucibles, and other apparatus of chemical research. An electrical machine stood ready for immediate use. The atmosphere felt oppressively close, and was tainted with gaseous odours, which had been tormented forth by the processes of science. The severe and homely simplicity of the apartment, with its naked walls and brick pavement, looked strange, accustomed as Georgiana had become to the fantastic elegance of her boudoir. But what chiefly, indeed almost solely, drew her attention, was the aspect of Aylmer himself.

He was pale as death, anxious, and absorbed, and hung over the furnace as if it depended upon his utmost watchfulness whether the liquid, which it was distilling, should be the draught of immortal happiness or misery. How different from the sanguine and joyous mien that he had assumed for Georgiana's encouragement!

"Carefully now, Aminadab! Carefully, thou human machine! Carefully, thou man of clay!" muttered Aylmer, more to himself than his assistant. "Now, if there be a thought too much or too little, it is all over!"

"Hoh! hoh!" mumbled Aminadab — "look, master, look!"

Aylmer raised his eyes hastily, and at first reddened, then grew paler than ever, on beholding Georgiana. He rushed towards her, and seized her arm with a grip that left the print of his fingers upon it.

"Why do you come hither? Have you no trust in your husband?" cried he impetuously. "Would you throw the blight of that fatal birth-mark over my labours? It is not well done. Go, prying woman, go!"

"Nay, Aylmer," said Georgiana, with the firmness of which she possessed no stinted endowment, "it is not you that have a right to complain. You mistrust your wife! You have concealed the anxiety with which you watch the development of this experiment. Think not so unworthily of me, my husband! Tell me all the risk we run; and fear not that I shall shrink, for my share in it is far less than your own!"

"No, no, Georgiana!" said Aylmer impatiently, "it must not be."

"I submit," replied she calmly. "And, Aylmer, I shall quaff whatever draught you bring me; but it will be on the same principle that would induce me to take a dose of poison, if offered by your hand."

"My noble wife," said Aylmer, deeply moved, "I knew not the height and depth of your nature, until now. Nothing shall be concealed. Know, then, that this Crimson Hand, superficial as it seems, has clutched its grasp into your being, with a strength of which I had no previous conception. I have already administered agents powerful enough to do aught except to change your entire physical system. Only one thing remains to be tried. If that fail us, we are ruined!"

"Why did you hesitate to tell me this?" asked she.

"Because, Georgiana," said Aylmer, in a low voice, "there is danger!"

"Danger? There is but one danger — that this horrible stigma shall be left upon my cheek!" cried Georgiana. "Remove it! remove it! — whatever be the cost — or we shall both go mad!"

"Heaven knows, your words are too true," said Aylmer, sadly. "And now, dearest, return to your boudoir. In a little while, all will be tested."

He conducted her back, and took leave of her with a solemn tenderness, which spoke far more than his words how much was now at stake. After his departure, Georgiana became wrapt in musings. She considered the character of Aylmer, and did it completer justice than at any previous moment. Her heart exulted, while it trembled, at his honourable love, so pure and lofty that it would accept nothing less than perfection, nor miserably make itself contented with an earthlier nature than he had dreamed of. She felt how much more precious was such a sentiment, than that meaner kind which would have borne with the imperfection for her sake, and have been guilty of treason to holy love, by degrading its perfect idea to the level of the actual. And, with her whole spirit, she prayed, that, for a single moment, she might satisfy his highest and deepest conception. Longer than one moment, she well knew, it could not be; for his spirit was ever on the march — ever ascending — and each instant required something that was beyond the scope of the instant before.

The sound of her husband's footsteps aroused her. He bore a crystal goblet, containing a liquor colourless as water, but bright enough to be the draught of immortality. Aylmer was pale; but it seemed rather the consequence of a highly wrought state of mind, and tension of spirit, than of fear or doubt.

"The concoction of the draught has been perfect," said he, in answer to Georgiana's look. "Unless all my science have deceived me, it cannot fail."

"Save on your account, my dearest Aylmer," observed his wife, "I might wish to put off this birthmark of mortality by relinquishing mortality itself, in preference to any other mode. Life is but a sad possession to those who have attained precisely the degree of moral advancement at which I stand. Were I weaker and blinder, it might be happiness. Were I stronger, it might be endured hopefully. But, being what I find myself, methinks I am of all mortals the most fit to die."

"You are fit for heaven without tasting death!" replied her husband. "But why do we speak of dying? The draught cannot fail. Behold its effect upon this plant!"

On the window-seat there stood a geranium, diseased with yellow blotches, which had overspread all its leaves. Aylmer poured a small quantity of the liquid upon the soil in which it grew. In a little time, when the roots of the plant had taken up the moisture, the unsightly blotches began to be extinguished in a living verdure.

"There needed no proof," said Georgiana, quietly. "Give me the goblet. I joyfully stake all upon your word."

"Drink, then, thou lofty creature!" exclaimed Aylmer, with fervid admiration. "There is no taint of imperfection on thy spirit. Thy sensible frame, too, shall soon be all perfect!"

She quaffed the liquid, and returned the goblet to his hand.

"It is grateful," said she, with a placid smile. "Methinks it is like water from a heavenly fountain; for it contains I know not what of unobtrusive fragrance and deliciousness. It allays a feverish thirst, that had parched me for many days. Now, dearest, let me sleep. My earthly senses are closing over my spirit, like the leaves around the heart of a rose, at sunset."

She spoke the last words with a gentle reluctance, as if it required almost more energy than she could command to pronounce the faint and lingering syllables. Scarcely had they loitered through her lips, ere she was lost in slumber. Aylmer sat by her side, watching her aspect with the emotions proper to a man, the whole value of whose existence was involved in the process now to be tested. Mingled with this mood, however, was the philosophic investigation, characteristic of the man of science. Not the minutest symptom escaped him. A heightened flush of the cheek — a slight irregularity of breath — a quiver of the eyelid — a hardly perceptible tremor through the frame — such were the details which, as the moments passed, he wrote down in his folio volume. Intense thought had set its stamp upon every previous page of that volume; but the thoughts of years were all concentrated upon the last.

While thus employed, he failed not to gaze often at the fatal Hand, and not without a shudder. Yet once, by a strange and unaccountable impulse, he pressed it with his lips. His spirit recoiled, however, in the very act, and Georgiana, out of the midst of her deep sleep, moved uneasily and murmured, as if in remonstrance. Again, Aylmer resumed his watch. Nor was it without avail. The Crimson Hand, which at first had been strongly visible upon the marble paleness of Georgiana's cheek now grew more faintly outlined. She remained not less pale than ever; but the birth-mark, with every breath that came and went, lost somewhat of its former distinctness. Its presence had been awful; its departure was more awful still. Watch the stain of the rainbow fading out of the sky; and you will know how that mysterious symbol passed away.

"By Heaven, it is well-nigh gone!" said Aylmer to himself, in almost irrepressible ecstasy. "I can scarcely trace it now. Success! Success! And now it is like the faintest rose-colour. The slightest flush of blood across her cheek would overcome it. But she is so pale!"

He drew aside the window-curtain, and suffered the light of natural day to fall into the room, and rest upon her cheek. At the same time, he heard a gross, hoarse chuckle, which he had long known as his servant Aminadab's expression of delight.

"Ah, clod! Ah, earthly mass!" cried Aylmer,

laughing in a sort of frenzy. "You have served me well! Matter and Spirit — Earth and Heaven — have both done their part in this! Laugh, thing of the senses! You have earned the right to laugh."

These exclamations broke Georgiana's sleep. She slowly unclosed her eyes, and gazed into the mirror, which her husband had arranged for that purpose. A faint smile flitted over her lips, when she recognized how barely perceptible was now that Crimson Hand, which had once blazed forth with such disastrous brilliancy as to scare away all their happiness. But then her eyes sought Aylmer's face, with a trouble and anxiety that he could by no means account for.

"My poor Aylmer!" murmured she.

"Poor? Nay, richest! Happiest! Most favoured!" exclaimed he. "My peerless bride, it is successful! You are perfect!"

"My poor Aylmer!" she repeated, with a more than human tenderness. "You have aimed loftily! — you have done nobly! Do not repent, that, with so high and pure a feeling, you have rejected the best the earth could offer. Aylmer — dearest Aylmer, I am dying!"

Alas, it was too true! The fatal Hand had grappled with the mystery of life, and was the bond by which an angelic spirit kept itself in union with a mortal frame. As the last crimson tint of the birthmark — that sole token of human imperfection — faded from her cheek, the parting breath of the now perfect woman passed into the atmosphere, and her soul, lingering a moment near her husband, took its heavenward flight. Then a hoarse, chuckling laugh was heard again! Thus ever does the gross Fatality of Earth exult in its invariable triumph over the immortal essence, which, in this dim sphere of half-development, demands the completeness of a higher state. Yet, had Aylmer reached a profounder wisdom, he need not thus have flung away the happiness, which would have woven his mortal life of the self-same texture with the celestial. The momentary circumstance was too strong for him; he failed to look beyond the shadowy scope of Time, and living once for all in Eternity, to find the perfect Future in the present.

V. A Terribly Strange Bed — Wilkie Collins

Shortly after my education at college was finished, I happened to be staying at Paris with an English friend. We were both young men then, and lived, I am afraid, rather a wild life, in the delightful city of our sojourn. One night we were idling about the neighbourhood of the Palais Royal, doubtful to what amusement we should next betake ourselves. My friend proposed a visit to Frascati's; but his suggestion was not to my taste. I knew Frascati's, as the French saying is, by heart; had lost and won plenty of five-franc pieces there, merely for amusement's sake, until it was amusement no longer, and was thoroughly tired, in fact, of all the ghastly respectabilities of such a social anomaly as a respectable gambling-house.

"For Heaven's sake," said I to my friend, "let us go somewhere where we can see a little genuine, blackguard, poverty-stricken gaming, with no false gingerbread glitter thrown over it at all. Let us get away from fashionable Frascati's, to a house where they don't mind letting in a man with a ragged coat, or a man with no coat, ragged or otherwise."

"Very well," said my friend, "we needn't go out of the Palais Royal to find the sort of company you want. Here's the place just before us; as blackguard a place, by all report, as you could possibly wish to see."

In another minute we arrived at the door, and entered the house.

When we got upstairs, and had left our hats and sticks with the doorkeeper, we were admitted into the chief gambling-room. We did not find many people assembled there. But, few as the men were who looked up at us on our entrance, they were all types — lamentably true types — of their respective classes.

We had come to see blackguards; but these men were something worse. There is a comic side, more or less appreciable, in all blackguardism: here there was nothing but tragedy — mute, weird tragedy. The quiet in the room was horrible. The thin, haggard, long-haired young man, whose sunken eyes fiercely watched the turning up of the cards, never spoke; the flabby, fat-faced, pimply player, who pricked his piece of pasteboard perseveringly, to register how often black won, and how often red, never spoke; the dirty, wrinkled old man, with the vulture eyes and the darned great-coat, who had lost his last sou, and still looked on desperately after he could play no longer, never spoke. Even the voice of the croupier sounded as if it were strangely dulled and thickened in the atmosphere of the room. I had entered the place to laugh, but the spectacle before me was something to weep over. I soon found it necessary to take refuge in excitement from the depression of spirits which was fast stealing on me. Unfortunately I sought the nearest excitement, by going to the table and beginning to play. Still more unfortunately, as the event will show, I won — won prodigiously; won incredibly; won at such a rate that the regular players at the table crowded round me; and staring at my stakes with hungry, superstitious eyes, whispered to one another that the English stranger was going to break the bank.

The game was Rouge et Noir. I had played at it in every city in Europe, without, however, the care or the wish to study the Theory of Chances — that philosopher's stone of all gamblers! And a gambler, in the strict sense of the word, I had never been. I was heart-whole from the corroding passion for play. My gaming was a mere idle amusement. I never resorted to it by necessity, because I never knew what it was to want money. I never practised it so incessantly as to lose more than I could afford, or to gain more than I could coolly pocket without being thrown off my balance by my good luck. In short, I had hitherto frequented gambling-tables — just as I frequented ball-rooms and opera-houses — because they amused me, and because I had nothing better to do with my leisure hours.

But on this occasion it was very different — now, for the first time in my life, I felt what the passion for play really was. My successes first bewildered, and then, in the most literal meaning of the word, intoxicated me. Incredible as it may appear, it is nevertheless true, that I only lost when I attempted to estimate chances, and played according to previous calculation. If I left everything to luck, and staked without any care or consideration, I was sure to win — to win in the face of every recognized probability in favour of the bank. At first some of the men present ventured their money safely enough on my colour; but I speedily increased my stakes to sums which they dared not risk. One after another they left off playing, and breathlessly looked on at my game.

Still, time after time, I staked higher and higher, and still won. The excitement in the room rose to fever pitch. The silence was interrupted by a deep-muttered chorus of oaths and exclamations in different languages, every time the gold was shovelled across to my side of the table — even the imperturbable croupier dashed his rake on the floor in a (French) fury of astonishment at my success. But one man present preserved his self-possession, and that man was my friend. He came to my side, and whispering in English, begged me to leave the place, satisfied with what I had already gained. I must do him the justice to say that he repeated his warnings and entreaties several times, and only left me and went away, after I had rejected his advice (I was to all intents and purposes gambling drunk) in terms which rendered it impossible for him to address me again that night.

Shortly after he had gone, a hoarse voice behind me cried, "Permit me, my dear sir — permit me to restore to their proper place two napoleons which you have dropped. Wonderful luck, sir! I pledge you my word of honour, as an old soldier, in the course of my long experience in this sort of thing, I never saw such luck as yours — never! Go on, sir — *Sacre mille bombes!* Go on boldly, and break the bank!"

I turned round and saw, nodding and smiling at me with inveterate civility, a tall man, dressed in a frogged and braided surtout.

If I had been in my senses, I should have considered him, personally, as being rather a suspicious specimen of an old soldier. He had goggling, bloodshot eyes, mangy moustaches, and a broken nose. His voice betrayed a barrack-room intonation of the worst order, and he had the dirtiest pair of hands I ever saw — even in France. These little personal peculiarities exercised, however, no repelling influence on me. In the mad excitement, the reckless triumph of that moment, I was ready to "fraternize" with anybody who encouraged me in my game. I accepted the old soldier's offered pinch of snuff; clapped him on the back, and swore he was the honestest fellow in the world — the most glorious relic of the Grand Army that I had ever met with. "Go on!" cried my military friend, snapping his fingers in ecstasy — "Go on, and win! Break the bank — *Mille tonnerres!* my gallant English comrade, break the bank!"

And I *did* go on — went on at such a rate, that in another quarter of an hour the croupier called out, "Gentlemen, the bank has discontinued for tonight." All the notes, and all the gold in that "bank," now lay in a heap under my hands; the whole floating capital of the gambling-house was waiting to pour into my pockets!

"Tie up the money in your pocket-handkerchief, my worthy sir," said the old soldier, as I wildly plunged my hands into my heap of gold. "Tie it up, as we used to tie up a bit of dinner in the Grand Army; your winnings are too heavy for any breeches-pockets that ever were sewed. There! that's it — shovel them in, notes and all! *Credie!* what luck! Stop! another napoleon on the floor. *Ah! sacre petit polisson de Napoleon!* have I found thee at last? Now then, sir — two tight double knots each way with your honourable permission, and the money's safe. Feel it! feel it, fortunate sir! hard and round as a cannon-ball — *A bas* if they had only fired such cannon-balls at us at Austerlitz — *nom d'une pipe!* if they only had! And now, as an ancient grenadier, as an ex-brave of the French army, what remains for me to do? I ask what? Simply this, to entreat my valued English friend to drink a bottle of champagne with me, and toast the goddess Fortune in foaming goblets before we part!"

"Excellent ex-brave! Convivial ancient grenadier! Champagne by all means! An English cheer for an old soldier! Hurrah! hurrah! Another English cheer for the goddess Fortune! Hurrah! hurrah! hurrah!"

"Bravo! the Englishman; the amiable, gracious Englishman, in whose veins circulates the vivacious blood of France! Another glass? *A bas!* — the bottle is empty! Never mind! *Vive le vin!* I, the old soldier, order another bottle, and half a pound of *bonbons* with it!"

"No, no, ex-brave; never — ancient grenadier! *Your* bottle last time; *my* bottle this! Behold it! Toast away! The French Army! the great Napoleon! the present company! the croupier! the honest croupier's wife and daughters — if he has any! the ladies generally! everybody in the world!"

By the time the second bottle of champagne was emptied, I felt as if I had been drinking liquid fire — my brain seemed all aflame. No excess in wine had ever had this effect on me before in my life. Was it the result of a stimulant acting upon my system when I was in a highly excited state? Was my stomach in a particularly disordered condition? Or was the champagne amazingly strong?

"Ex-brave of the French Army!" cried I, in a mad state of exhilaration, "*I* am on fire! how are *you*? You have set me on fire! Do you hear, my hero of Austerlitz? Let us have a third bottle of champagne to put the flame out!"

The old soldier wagged his head, rolled his goggle-eyes, until I expected to see them slip out of their sockets; placed his dirty forefinger by the side of his broken nose; solemnly ejaculated "Coffee!" and immediately ran off into an inner room.

The word pronounced by the eccentric veteran seemed to have a magical effect on the rest of the company present. With one accord they all rose to depart. Probably they had expected to profit by my intoxication; but finding that my new friend was benevolently bent on preventing me from getting dead drunk, had now abandoned all hope of thriving pleasantly on my winnings. Whatever their motive might be, at any rate they went away in a body. When the old soldier returned, and sat down again opposite to me at the table, we had the room to ourselves. I could see the croupier, in a sort of vestibule which opened out of it, eating his supper in solitude. The silence was now deeper than ever.

A sudden change, too, had come over the "ex-brave." He assumed a portentously solemn look; and when he spoke to me again, his speech was ornamented by no oaths, enforced by no finger-snapping, enlivened by no apostrophes or exclamations.

"Listen, my dear sir," said he, in mysteriously confidential tones — "listen to an old soldier's advice. I have been to the mistress of the house (a very charming woman, with a genius for cookery!) to impress on her the necessity of making us some particularly strong and good coffee. You must drink this coffee in order to get rid of your little amiable exaltation of spirits before you think of going home — you *must*, my good and gracious friend! With all that money to take home to-night, it is a sacred duty to yourself to have your wits about you. You are known to be a winner to an enormous extent by several gentlemen present to-night, who, in a certain point of view, are very worthy and excellent fellows; but they are mortal men, my dear sir, and they have their amiable weaknesses! Need I say more? Ah, no, no! you understand me! Now, this is what you must do — send for a cabriolet when you feel quite well again — draw up all the windows when you get into it — and tell the driver to take you home only through the large and well-lighted thoroughfares. Do this; and you and your money will be safe. Do this; and to-morrow you will thank an old soldier for giving you a word of honest advice."

Just as the ex-brave ended his oration in very lachrymose tones, the coffee came in, ready poured out in two cups. My attentive friend handed me one of the cups with a bow. I was parched with thirst, and drank it off at a draft. Almost instantly afterward I was seized with a fit of giddiness, and felt more completely intoxicated than ever. The room whirled round and round furiously; the old soldier seemed to be regularly bobbing up and down before me like the piston of a steam-engine. I was half deafened by a violent singing in my ears; a feeling of utter bewilderment, helplessness, idiocy, overcame me. I rose from my chair, holding on by the table to keep my balance; and stammered out that I felt dreadfully unwell — so unwell that I did not know how I was to get home.

"My dear friend," answered the old soldier — and even his voice seemed to be bobbing up and down as he spoke — "my dear friend, it would be madness to go home in *your* state; you would be sure to lose your money; you might be robbed and murdered with the greatest ease. *I* am going to sleep here: *do* you sleep here, too — they make up capital beds in this house — take one; sleep off the effects of the wine, and go home safely with your winnings to-morrow — to-morrow, in broad daylight."

I had but two ideas left: one, that I must never let go hold of my handkerchief full of money; the other, that I must lie down somewhere immediately, and fall off into a comfortable sleep. So I agreed to the proposal about the bed, and took the offered arm of the old soldier, carrying my money with my disengaged hand. Preceded by the croupier, we passed along some passages and up a flight of stairs into the bedroom which I was to occupy. The ex-brave shook me warmly by the hand, proposed that we should breakfast together, and then, followed by the croupier, left me for the night.

I ran to the wash-hand stand; drank some of the water in my jug; poured the rest out, and plunged my face into it; then sat down in a chair and tried to compose myself. I soon felt better. The change for my lungs, from the fetid atmosphere of the gambling-room to the cool air of the apartment I now occupied, the almost equally refreshing change for my eyes, from the glaring gaslights of the "salon" to the dim, quiet flicker of one bedroom-candle, aided wonderfully the restorative effects of cold water. The giddiness left me, and I began to feel a little like a reasonable being again. My first thought was of the risk of sleeping all night in a gambling-house; my second, of the still greater risk of trying to get out after the house was closed, and of going home alone at night through the streets of Paris with a large sum of money about me. I had slept in worse places than this on my travels; so I determined to lock, bolt, and barricade my door, and take my chance till the next morning.

Accordingly, I secured myself against all intrusion; looked under the bed, and into the cupboard; tried the fastening of the window; and then, satisfied that I had taken every proper precaution, pulled off my upper clothing, put my light, which was a dim one, on the hearth among a feathery litter of wood-ashes, and got into bed, with the handkerchief full of money under my pillow.

I soon felt not only that I could not go to sleep, but that I could not even close my eyes. I was wide awake, and in a high fever. Every nerve in my body trembled — every one of my senses seemed to be preternaturally sharpened. I tossed and rolled, and tried every kind of position, and perseveringly sought out the cold corners of the bed, and all to no purpose. Now I thrust my arms over the clothes; now I poked them under the clothes; now I violently shot my legs straight out down to the bottom of the bed; now I convulsively coiled them up as near my chin as they would go; now I shook out my crumpled pillow, changed it to the cool side, patted it flat, and lay down quietly on my back; now I fiercely doubled it in two, set it up on end, thrust it against the board of the bed, and tried a sitting posture. Every effort was in vain; I groaned with vexation as I felt that I was in for a sleepless night.

What could I do? I had no book to read. And yet, unless I found out some method of diverting my mind, I felt certain that I was in the condition to imagine all sorts of horrors; to rack my brain with forebodings of every possible and impossible danger; in short, to pass the night in suffering all conceivable varieties of nervous terror.

I raised myself on my elbow, and looked about the room — which was brightened by a lovely moonlight pouring straight through the window — to see if it contained any pictures or ornaments that I could at all clearly distinguish. While my eyes wandered from wall to wall, a remembrance of Le Maistre's delightful little book, "Voyage autour de ma Chambre," occurred to me. I resolved to imitate the French author, and find occupation and amusement enough to relieve the tedium of my wakefulness, by making a mental inventory of every article of furniture I could see, and by following up to their sources the multitude of associations which even a chair, a table, or a wash-hand stand may be made to call forth.

In the nervous, unsettled state of my mind at that moment, I found it much easier to make my inventory than to make my reflections, and thereupon soon gave up all hope of thinking in Le Maistre's fanciful track — or, indeed, of thinking at all. I looked about the room at the different articles of furniture, and did nothing more.

There was, first, the bed I was lying in; a four-post bed, of all things in the world to meet with in Paris — yes, a thorough clumsy British four-poster, with a regular top lined with chintz — the regular fringed valance all round — the regular stifling, unwholesome curtains, which I remembered having mechanically drawn back against the posts without particularly noticing the bed when I first got into the room. Then there was the marble-topped wash-hand stand, from which the water I had spilled, in my hurry to pour it out, was still dripping, slowly and more slowly, on to the brick floor. Then two small chairs, with my coat, waistcoat, and trousers flung on them. Then a large elbow-chair covered with dirty white dimity, with my cravat and shirt collar thrown over the back. Then a chest of drawers with two of the brass handles off, and a tawdry, broken china inkstand placed on it by way of ornament for the top. Then the dressing-table, adorned by a very small looking-glass, and a very large pincushion. Then the window — an unusually large window. Then a dark old picture, which the feeble candle dimly showed me. It was the picture of a fellow in a high Spanish hat, crowned with a plume of towering feathers. A swarthy, sinister ruffian, looking upward, shading his eyes with his hand, and looking intently upward — it might be at some tall gallows on which he was going to be hanged. At any rate, he had the appearance of thoroughly deserving it.

This picture put a kind of constraint upon me to look upward too — at the top of the bed. It was a gloomy and not an interesting object, and I looked back at the picture. I counted the feathers in the man's hat — they stood out in relief — three white, two green. I observed the crown of his hat, which was of a conical shape, according to the fashion supposed to have been favoured by Guido Fawkes. I wondered what he was looking up at. It couldn't be at the stars; such a desperado was neither astrologer nor astronomer. It must be at the high gallows, and he was going to be hanged presently. Would the executioner come into possession of his conical crowned hat and plume of feathers? I counted the feathers again — three white, two green.

While I still lingered over this very improving and intellectual employment, my thoughts insensibly began to wander. The moonlight shining into the room reminded me of a certain moonlight night in England — the night after a picnic party in a Welsh valley. Every incident of the drive homeward through lovely scenery, which the moonlight made lovelier than ever, came back to my remembrance, though I had never given the picnic a thought for years; though, if I had *tried* to recollect it, I could certainly have recalled little or nothing of that scene long past. Of all the wonderful faculties that help to tell us we are immortal, which speaks the sublime truth more eloquently than memory? Here was I, in a strange house of the most suspicious character, in a situation of uncertainty, and even of peril, which might seem to make the cool exercise of my recollection almost out of the question; nevertheless, remembering, quite involuntarily, places, people, conversations, minute circumstances of every kind, which I had thought forgotten forever; which I could not possibly have recalled at will, even under the most favourable auspices. And what cause had produced in a moment the whole of this strange, complicated, mysterious effect? Nothing but some rays of moonlight shining in at my bedroom window.

I was still thinking of the picnic — of our merriment on the drive home — of the sentimental young lady who *would* quote "Childe Harold" because it was moonlight. I was absorbed by these past scenes and past amusements, when, in an instant, the thread on which my memories hung snapped asunder; my attention immediately came back to present things more vividly than ever, and I found myself, I neither knew why nor wherefore, looking hard at the picture again.

Looking for what?

Good God! the man had pulled his hat down on his brows! No! the hat itself was gone! Where was the conical crown? Where the feathers — three white, two green? Not there! In place of the hat and feathers, what dusky object was it that now hid his forehead, his eyes, his shading hand?

Was the bed moving?

I turned on my back and looked up. Was I mad? drunk? dreaming? giddy again? or was the top of the bed really moving down — sinking slowly, regularly, silently, horribly, right down throughout the whole of its length and breadth — right down upon me, as I lay underneath?

My blood seemed to stand still. A deadly, paralyzing coldness stole all over me as I turned my head round on the pillow and determined to test whether the bed-top was really moving or not, by keeping my eye on the man in the picture.

The next look in that direction was enough. The dull, black, frowzy outline of the valance above me was within an inch of being parallel with his waist. I still looked breathlessly. And steadily and slowly — very slowly — I saw the figure, and the line of frame below the figure, vanish, as the valance moved down before it.

I am, constitutionally, anything but timid. I have been on more than one occasion in peril of my life, and have not lost my self-possession for an instant; but when the conviction first settled on my mind that the bed-top was really moving, was steadily and continuously sinking down upon me, I looked up shuddering, helpless, panic-stricken, beneath the hideous machinery for murder, which was advancing closer and closer to suffocate me where I lay.

I looked up, motionless, speechless, breathless. The candle, fully spent, went out; but the moonlight still brightened the room. Down and down, without pausing and without sounding, came the bed-top, and still my panic terror seemed to bind me faster and faster to the mattress on which I lay — down and down it sank, till the dusty odour from the lining of the canopy came stealing into my nostrils.

At that final moment the instinct of self-preservation startled me out of my trance, and I moved at last. There was just room for me to roll myself sidewise off the bed. As I dropped noiselessly to the floor, the edge of the murderous canopy touched me on the shoulder.

Without stopping to draw my breath, without wiping the cold sweat from my face, I rose instantly on my knees to watch the bed-top. I was literally spellbound by it. If I had heard footsteps behind me, I could not have turned round; if a means of escape had been miraculously provided for me, I could not have moved to take advantage of it. The whole life in me was, at that moment, concentrated in my eyes.

It descended — the whole canopy, with the fringe round it, came down — down — close down; so close that there was not room now to squeeze my finger between the bed-top and the bed. I felt at the side, and discovered that what had appeared to me from beneath to be the ordinary light canopy of a four-post bed was in reality a thick, broad mattress, the substance of which was concealed by the valance and its fringe. I looked up and saw the four posts rising hideously bare. In the middle of the bed-top was a huge wooden screw that had evidently worked it down through a hole in the ceiling, just as ordinary presses are worked down on the substance selected for compression. The frightful apparatus moved without making the faintest noise. There had been no creaking as it came down; there was now not the faintest sound from the room above. Amidst a dead and awful silence I beheld before me — in the nineteenth century, and in the civilized capital of France — such a machine for secret murder by suffocation as might have existed in the worst days of the Inquisition, in the lonely inns among the Hartz Mountains, in the mysterious tribunals of Westphalia! Still, as I looked on it, I could not move, I could hardly breathe, but I began to recover the power of thinking, and in a moment I discovered the murderous conspiracy framed against me in all its horror.

My cup of coffee had been drugged, and drugged too strongly. I had been saved from being smothered by having taken an overdose of some narcotic. How I had chafed and fretted at the fever fit which had preserved my life by keeping me awake! How recklessly I had confided myself to the two wretches who had led me into this room, determined, for the sake of my winnings, to kill me in my sleep by the surest and most horrible contrivance for secretly accomplishing my destruction! How many men, winners like me, had slept, as I had proposed to sleep, in that bed, and had never been seen or heard of more! I shuddered at the bare idea of it.

But ere long all thought was again suspended by the sight of the murderous canopy moving once more. After it had remained on the bed — as nearly as I could guess — about ten minutes, it began to move up again. The villains who worked it from above evidently believed that their purpose was now accomplished. Slowly and silently, as it had descended, that horrible bed-top rose toward its former place. When it reached the upper extremities of the four posts, it reached the ceiling too. Neither hole nor screw could be seen; the bed became in appearance an ordinary bed again — the canopy an ordinary canopy — even to the most suspicious eyes.

Now, for the first time, I was able to move — to

rise from my knees — to dress myself in my upper clothing — and to consider of how I should escape. If I betrayed by the smallest noise that the attempt to suffocate me had failed, I was certain to be murdered. Had I made any noise already? I listened intently, looking toward the door.

No! no footsteps in the passage outside — no sound of a tread, light or heavy, in the room above — absolute silence everywhere. Besides locking and bolting my door, I had moved an old wooden chest against it, which I had found under the bed. To remove this chest (my blood ran cold as I thought of what its contents *might* be!) without making some disturbance was impossible; and, moreover, to think of escaping through the house, now barred up for the night, was sheer insanity. Only one chance was left me — the window. I stole to it on tiptoe.

My bedroom was on the first floor, above an entresol, and looked into the back street. I raised my hand to open the window, knowing that on that action hung, by the merest hair-breadth, my chance of safety. They keep vigilant watch in a House of Murder. If any part of the frame cracked, if the hinge creaked, I was a lost man! It must have occupied me at least five minutes, reckoning by time — five *hours* reckoning by suspense — to open that window. I succeeded in doing it silently — in doing it with all the dexterity of a house-breaker — and then looked down into the street. To leap the distance beneath me would be almost certain destruction! Next, I looked round at the sides of the house. Down the left side ran a thick water-pipe — it passed close by the outer edge of the window. The moment I saw the pipe, I knew I was saved. My breath came and went freely for the first time since I had seen the canopy of the bed moving down upon me!

To some men the means of escape which I had discovered might have seemed difficult and dangerous enough — to *me* the prospect of slipping down the pipe into the street did not suggest even a thought of peril. I had always been accustomed, by the practise of gymnastics, to keep up my schoolboy powers as a daring and expert climber; and knew that my head, hands, and feet would serve me faithfully in any hazards of ascent or descent. I had already got one leg over the window-sill, when I remembered the handkerchief filled with money under my pillow. I could well have afforded to leave it behind me, but I was revengefully determined that the miscreants of the gambling-house should miss their plunder as well as their victim. So I went back to the bed and tied the heavy handkerchief at my back by my cravat.

Just as I had made it tight and fixed it in a comfortable place, I thought I heard a sound of breathing outside the door. The chill feeling of horror ran through me again as I listened. No! dead silence still in the passage — I had only heard the night air blowing softly into the room. The next moment I was on the window-sill — and the next I had a firm grip on the water-pipe with my hands and knees.

I slid down into the street easily and quietly, as I thought I should, and immediately set off at the top of my speed to a branch "Prefecture" of Police, which I knew was situated in the immediate neighbourhood. A "Sub-prefect," and several picked men among his subordinates, happened to be up, maturing, I believe, some scheme for discovering the perpetrator of a mysterious murder which all Paris was talking of just then. When I began my story, in a breathless hurry and in very bad French, I could see that the Sub-prefect suspected me of being a drunken Englishman who had robbed somebody; but he soon altered his opinion as I went on, and before I had anything like concluded, he shoved all the papers before him into a drawer, put on his hat, supplied me with another (for I was bareheaded), ordered a file of soldiers, desired his expert followers to get ready all sorts of tools for breaking open doors and ripping up brick flooring, and took my arm, in the most friendly and familiar manner possible, to lead me with him out of the house. I will venture to say that when the Sub-prefect was a little boy, and was taken for the first time to the play, he was not half as much pleased as he was now at the job in prospect for him at the gambling-house!

Away we went through the streets, the Sub-prefect cross-examining and congratulating me in the same breath as we marched at the head of our formidable *posse comitatus*. Sentinels were placed at the back and front of the house the moment we got to it, a tremendous battery of knocks was directed against the door; a light appeared at a window; I was told to conceal myself behind the police — then came more knocks, and a cry of "Open in the name of the law!" At that terrible summons bolts and locks gave way before an invisible hand, and the moment after the Sub-prefect was in the passage, confronting a waiter half dressed and ghastly pale. This was the short dialogue which immediately took place:

"We want to see the Englishman who is sleeping in this house."

"He went away hours ago."

"He did no such thing. His friend went away;

he remained. Show us to his bedroom!"

"I swear to you, Monsieur le Sous-prefect, he is not here! he — "

"I swear to you, Monsieur le Garçon, he is. He slept here — he didn't find your bed comfortable — he came to us to complain of it — here he is among my men — and here am I ready to look for a flea or two in his bedstead. Renaudin! (calling to one of the subordinates, and pointing to the waiter), collar that man, and tie his hands behind him. Now, then, gentlemen, let us walk upstairs!"

Every man and woman in the house was secured — the "Old Soldier" the first. Then I identified the bed in which I had slept, and then we went into the room above.

No object that was at all extraordinary appeared in any part of it. The Sub-prefect looked round the place, commanded everybody to be silent, stamped twice on the floor, called for a candle, looked attentively at the spot he had stamped on, and ordered the flooring there to be carefully taken up. This was done in no time. Lights were produced, and we saw a deep raftered cavity between the floor of this room and the ceiling of the room beneath. Through this cavity there ran perpendicularly a sort of case of iron thickly greased; and inside the case appeared the screw, which communicated with the bed-top below. Extra lengths of screw, freshly oiled; levers covered with felt; all the complete upper works of a heavy press — constructed with infernal ingenuity so as to join the fixtures below, and when taken to pieces again to go into the smallest possible compass — were next discovered and pulled out on the floor. After some little difficulty the Sub-prefect succeeded in putting the machinery together, and, leaving his men to work it, descended with me to the bedroom. The smothering canopy was then lowered, but not so noiselessly as I had seen it lowered. When I mentioned this to the Sub-prefect, his answer, simple as it was, had a terrible significance. "My men," said he, "are working down the bed-top for the first time — the men whose money you won were in better practise."

We left the house in the sole possession of two police agents — every one of the inmates being removed to prison on the spot. The Sub-prefect, after taking down my "procès verbal" in his office, returned with me to my hotel to get my passport. "Do you think," I asked, as I gave it to him, "that any men have really been smothered in that bed, as they tried to smother *me*?"

"I have seen dozens of drowned men laid out at the Morgue," answered the Sub-prefect, "in whose pocketbooks were found letters stating that they had committed suicide in the Seine, because they had lost everything at the gaming-table. Do I know how many of those men entered the same gambling-house that *you* entered? won as *you* won? took that bed as *you* took it? slept in it? were smothered in it? and were privately thrown into the river, with a letter of explanation written by the murderers and placed in their pocketbooks? No man can say how many or how few have suffered the fate from which you have escaped. The people of the gambling house kept their bedstead machinery a secret from us — even from the police! The dead kept the rest of the secret for them. Good-night, or rather good-morning, Monsieur Faulkner! Be at my office again at nine o'clock — in the meantime, au revoir!"

The rest of my story is soon told. I was examined and reexamined; the gambling-house was strictly searched all through from top to bottom; the prisoners were separately interrogated; and two of the less guilty among them made a confession. I discovered that the Old Soldier was the master of the gambling-house — *justice* discovered that he had been drummed out of the army as a vagabond years ago; that he had been guilty of all sorts of villainies since; that he was in possession of stolen property, which the owners identified; and that he, the croupier, another accomplice, and the woman who had made my cup of coffee, were all in the secret of the bedstead. There appeared some reason to doubt whether the inferior persons attached to the house knew anything of the suffocating machinery; and they received the benefit of that doubt, by being treated simply as thieves and vagabonds. As for the Old Soldier and his two head myrmidons, they went to the galleys; the woman who had drugged my coffee was imprisoned for I forget how many years; the regular attendants at the gambling-house were considered "suspicious," and placed under "surveillance"; and I became, for one whole week (which is a long time), the head "lion" in Parisian society. My adventure was dramatized by three illustrious play-makers, but never saw theatrical daylight; for the censorship forbade the introduction on the stage of a correct copy of the gambling-house bedstead.

One good result was produced by my adventure, which any censorship must have approved: it cured me of ever again trying "Rouge et Noir" as an amusement. The sight of a green cloth, with packs of cards and heaps of money on it, will henceforth be forever associated in my mind with the sight of a bed canopy descending to suffocate me in the silence and darkness of the night.

VI. The Torture by Hope — Villiers de l'Isle Adam

Many years ago, as evening was closing in, the venerable Pedro Arbuez d'Espila, sixth prior of the Dominicans of Segovia, and third Grand Inquisitor of Spain, followed by a *fra redemptor*, and preceded by two familiars of the Holy Office, the latter carrying lanterns, made their way to a subterranean dungeon. The bolt of a massive door creaked, and they entered a mephitic *in-pace*, where the dim light revealed between rings fastened to the wall a blood-stained rack, a brazier, and a jug. On a pile of straw, loaded with fetters and his neck encircled by an iron carcan, sat a haggard man, of uncertain age, clothed in rags.

This prisoner was no other than Rabbi Aser Abarbanel, a Jew of Arragon, who — accused of usury and pitiless scorn for the poor — had been daily subjected to torture for more than a year. Yet "his blindness was as dense as his hide," and he had refused to abjure his faith.

Proud of a filiation dating back thousands of years, proud of his ancestors — for all Jews worthy of the name are vain of their blood — he descended Talmudically from Othoniel and consequently from Ipsiboa, the wife of the last judge of Israel, a circumstance which had sustained his courage amid incessant torture. With tears in his eyes at the thought of this resolute soul rejecting salvation, the venerable Pedro Arbuez d'Espila, approaching the shuddering rabbi, addressed him as follows:

"My son, rejoice: your trials here below are about to end. If in the presence of such obstinacy I was forced to permit, with deep regret, the use of great severity, my task of fraternal correction has its limits. You are the fig tree which, having failed so many times to bear fruit, at last withered, but God alone can judge your soul. Perhaps Infinite Mercy will shine upon you at the last moment! We must hope so. There are examples. So sleep in peace tonight. To-morrow you will be included in the *auto da fé*: that is, you will be exposed to the *quéma-dero*, the symbolical flames of the Everlasting Fire: It burns, as you know, only at a distance, my son; and Death is at least two hours (often three) in coming, on account of the wet, iced bandages, with which we protect the heads and hearts of the condemned. There will be forty-three of you. Placed in the last row, you will have time to invoke God and offer to Him this baptism of fire, which is of the Holy Spirit. Hope in the Light, and rest."

With these words, having signed to his companions to unchain the prisoner, the prior tenderly embraced him. Then came the turn of the *fra redemptor*, who, in a low tone, entreated the Jew's forgiveness for what he had made him suffer for the purpose of redeeming him; then the two familiars silently kissed him. This ceremony over, the captive was left, solitary and bewildered, in the darkness.

*****

Rabbi Aser Abarbanel, with parched lips and visage worn by suffering, at first gazed at the closed door with vacant eyes. Closed? The word unconsciously roused a vague fancy in his mind, the fancy that he had seen for an instant the light of the lanterns through a chink between the door and the wall. A morbid idea of hope, due to the weakness of his brain, stirred his whole being. He dragged himself toward the strange *appearance*. Then, very gently and cautiously, slipping one finger into the crevice, he drew the door toward him. Marvellous! By an extraordinary accident the familiar who closed it had turned the huge key an instant before it struck the stone casing, so that the rusty bolt not having entered the hole, the door again rolled on its hinges.

The rabbi ventured to glance outside. By the aid of a sort of luminous dusk he distinguished at first a semicircle of walls indented by winding stairs; and opposite to him, at the top of five or six stone steps, a sort of black portal, opening into an immense corridor, whose first arches only were visible from below.

Stretching himself flat he crept to the threshold. Yes, it was really a corridor, but endless in length. A wan light illumined it: lamps suspended from the vaulted ceiling lightened at intervals the dull hue of the atmosphere — the distance was veiled in shadow. Not a single door appeared in the whole extent! Only on one side, the left, heavily grated loopholes sunk in the walls, admitted a light which must be that of evening, for crimson bars at intervals rested on the flags of the pavement. What a terrible silence! Yet, yonder, at the far end of that passage there might be a doorway of escape! The Jew's vacillating hope was tenacious, for it was *the last*.

Without hesitating, he ventured on the flags, keeping close under the loopholes, trying to make himself part of the blackness of the long walls. He advanced slowly, dragging himself along on his breast, forcing back the cry of pain when some raw wound sent a keen pang through his whole body.

Suddenly the sound of a sandaled foot approaching reached his ears. He trembled violently, fear stifled him, his sight grew dim. Well, it was over, no doubt. He pressed himself into a niche and half lifeless with terror, waited.

It was a familiar hurrying along. He passed swiftly by, holding in his clenched hand an instrument of torture — a frightful figure — and vanished. The suspense which the rabbi had endured seemed to have suspended the functions of life, and he lay nearly an hour unable to move. Fearing an increase of tortures if he were captured, he thought of returning to his dungeon. But the old hope whispered in his soul that divine *perhaps*, which comforts us in our sorest trials. A miracle had happened. He could doubt no longer. He began to crawl toward the chance of escape. Exhausted by suffering and hunger, trembling with pain, he pressed onward. The sepulchral corridor seemed to lengthen mysteriously, while he, still advancing, gazed into the gloom where there *must* be some avenue of escape.

Oh! oh! He again heard footsteps, but this time they were slower, more heavy. The white and black forms of two inquisitors appeared, emerging from the obscurity beyond. They were conversing in low tones, and seemed to be discussing some important subject, for they were gesticulating vehemently.

At this spectacle Rabbi Aser Abarbanel closed his eyes: his heart beat so violently that it almost suffocated him; his rags were damp with the cold sweat of agony; he lay motionless by the wall, his mouth wide open, under the rays of a lamp, praying to the God of David.

Just opposite to him the two inquisitors paused under the light of the lamp — doubtless owing to some accident due to the course of their argument. One, while listening to his companion, gazed at the rabbi! And, beneath the look — whose absence of expression the hapless man did not at first notice —

he fancied he again felt the burning pincers scorch his flesh, he was to be once more a living wound. Fainting, breathless, with fluttering eyelids, he shivered at the touch of the monk's floating robe. But — strange yet natural fact — the inquisitor's gaze was evidently that of a man deeply absorbed in his intended reply, engrossed by what he was hearing; his eyes were fixed — and seemed to look at the Jew *without seeing him*.

In fact, after the lapse of a few minutes, the two gloomy figures slowly pursued their way, still conversing in low tones, toward the place whence the prisoner had come; HE HAD NOT BEEN SEEN! Amid the horrible confusion of the rabbi's thoughts, the idea darted through his brain: "Can I be already dead that they did not see me?" A hideous impression roused him from his lethargy: in looking at the wall against which his face was pressed, he imagined he beheld two fierce eyes watching him! He flung his head back in a sudden frenzy of fright, his hair fairly bristling! Yet, no! No. His hand groped over the stones: it was the *reflection* of the inquisitor's eyes, still retained in his own, which had been refracted from two spots on the wall.

Forward! He must hasten toward that goal which he fancied (absurdly, no doubt) to be deliverance, toward the darkness from which he was now barely thirty paces distant. He pressed forward faster on his knees, his hands, at full length, dragging himself painfully along, and soon entered the dark portion of this terrible corridor.

Suddenly the poor wretch felt a gust of cold air on the hands resting upon the flags; it came from under the little door to which the two walls led.

Oh, Heaven, if that door should open outward.

Every nerve in the miserable fugitive's body thrilled with hope. He examined it from top to bottom, though scarcely able to distinguish its outlines in the surrounding darkness. He passed his hand over it: no bolt, no lock! A latch! He started up, the latch yielded to the pressure of his thumb: the door silently swung open before him.

*****

"Halleluia!" murmured the rabbi in a transport of gratitude as, standing on the threshold, he beheld the scene before him.

The door had opened into the gardens, above which arched a starlit sky, into spring, liberty, life! It revealed the neighbouring fields, stretching toward the sierras, whose sinuous blue lines were relieved against the horizon. Yonder lay freedom! O, to escape! He would journey all night through the lemon groves, whose fragrance reached him. Once in the mountains and he was safe! He inhaled the delicious air; the breeze revived him, his lungs expanded! He felt in his swelling heart the *Veni foràs* of Lazarus! And to thank once more the God who had bestowed this mercy upon him, he extended his arms, raising his eyes toward Heaven. It was an ecstasy of joy!

Then he fancied he saw the shadow of his arms approach him — fancied that he felt these shadowy arms inclose, embrace him — and that he was pressed tenderly to some one's breast. A tall figure actually did stand directly before him. He lowered his eyes — and remained motionless, gasping for breath, dazed, with fixed eyes, fairly drivelling with terror.

Horror! He was in the clasp of the Grand Inquisitor himself, the venerable Pedro Arbuez d'Espila who gazed at him with tearful eyes, like a good shepherd who had found his stray lamb.

The dark-robed priest pressed the hapless Jew to his heart with so fervent an outburst of love, that the edges of the monochal haircloth rubbed the Dominican's breast. And while Aser Abarbanel with protruding eyes gasped in agony in the ascetic's embrace, vaguely comprehending that all the phases of this fatal evening were only a prearranged torture, that of Hope, the Grand Inquisitor, with an accent of touching reproach and a look of consternation, murmured in his ear, his breath parched and burning from long fasting:

"What, my son! On the eve, perchance, of salvation — you wished to leave us?"

VII. The Box with the Iron Clamps — Florence Marryat

I

Molton Chase is a charming, old-fashioned country house, which has been in the possession of the Clayton family for centuries past; and as Harry Clayton, its present owner, has plenty of money, and (having tasted the pleasures of matrimony for only five years) has no knowledge (as yet) of the delights of college and school bills coming in at Christmas-time, it is his will to fill the Chase at that season with guests, to each of whom he extends a welcome, as hearty as it is sincere.

"Bella! are you not going to join the riding-party this afternoon?" he said across the luncheon-table to his wife, one day in a December not long ago.

"Bella" was a dimpled little woman, whose artless expression of countenance would well bear comparison with the honest, genial face opposite to her, and who replied at once —

"No! not this afternoon, Harry, dear. You know the Damers may come at any time between this and seven o'clock, and I should not like to be out when they arrive."

"And may I ask Mrs. Clayton who *are* the Damers," inquired a friend of her husband, who, on account of being handsome, considered himself licensed to be pert — "that their advent should be the cause of our losing the pleasure of your company this afternoon?"

But the last thing Bella Clayton ever did was to take offence.

"The Damers are my cousins, Captain Moss," she replied; "at least Blanche Damer is."

At this juncture a dark-eyed man who was sitting at the other end of the table dropped the flirting converse he had been maintaining with a younger sister of Mrs. Clayton's, and appeared to become interested in what his hostess was saying.

"Colonel Damer," he continued, "has been in India for the last twelve years, and only returned to England a month ago; therefore it would seem unkind on the first visit he has paid to his relatives that there should be no one at home to welcome him."

"Has Mrs. Damer been abroad for as long a time?" resumed her questioner, a vision arising on his mental faculties of a lemon-coloured woman with shoes down at heel.

"Oh dear no!" replied his hostess. "Blanche came to England about five years ago, but her health has been too delicate to rejoin her husband in India since. Have we all finished, Harry, dear?" — and in another minute the luncheon-table was cleared.

As Mrs. Clayton crossed the hall soon afterwards to visit her nursery, the same dark-eyed man who had regarded her fixedly when she mentioned the name of Blanche Damer followed and accosted her.

"Is it long since you have seen your cousin Mrs. Damer, Mrs. Clayton?"

"I saw her about three years ago, Mr. Laurence; but she had a severe illness soon after that, and has been living on the Continent ever since. Why do you ask?"

"For no especial reason," he answered smiling. "Perhaps I am a little jealous lest this new-comer to whose arrival you look forward with so much interest should usurp more of your time and attention than we less-favoured ones can spare."

He spoke with a degree of sarcasm, real or feigned, which Mrs. Clayton immediately resented.

"I am not aware that I have been in the habit of neglecting my guests, Mr. Laurence," she replied; "but my cousin Blanche is more likely to remind me of my duties than to tempt me to forget them."

"Forgive me," he said, earnestly. "You have mistaken my meaning altogether. But are you very intimate with this lady?"

"Very much so," was the answer. "We were brought up together, and loved each other as sisters until she married and went to India. For some years after her return home our intercourse was renewed, and only broken, on the occasion of her being ill and going abroad, as I have described to you. Her husband, I have, of course, seen less of, but I like what I know of him, and am anxious to show them both all the hospitality in my power. She is a charming creature, and I am sure you will admire her."

"Doubtless I shall," he replied; "that is if she does not lay claim to all Mrs. Clayton's interest in the affairs of Molton Chase."

"No fear of that," laughed the cheery little lady as she ascended the stairs, and left Mr. Laurence standing in the hall beneath.

"Clayton," observed that gentleman, as he re-entered the luncheon-room and drew his host into the privacy of a bay-window, "I really am afraid I shall have to leave you this evening — if you won't think it rude of me to go so suddenly."

"But *why*, my dear fellow?" exclaimed Harry Clayton, as his blue eyes searched into the other's soul. "What earthly reason can you have for going, when your fixed plan was to stay with us over Christmas Day?"

"Well! there is lots of work waiting for me to do, you know; and really the time slips away so, and time is money to a slave like myself — that — "

"Now, my dear Laurence," said Harry Clayton conclusively, "you know you are only making excuses. All the work that was absolutely necessary for you to do before Christmas was finished before you came here, and you said you felt yourself licensed to take a whole month's holiday. Now, was not that the case?"

Mr. Laurence could not deny the fact, and so he looked undecided, and was silent.

"Don't let me hear any more about your going before Christmas Day," said his host, "or I shall be offended, and so will Bella; to say nothing of Bella's sister — eh, Laurence!"

Whereupon Mr. Laurence felt himself bound to remain; and saying in his own mind that fate was against him, dropped the subject of his departure altogether.

One hour later, the riding party being then some miles from Molton Chase, a travelling carriage laden with trunks drove up to the house, and Mrs. Clayton, all blushes and smiles, stood on the hall-steps to welcome her expected guests.

Colonel Damer was the first to alight. He was a

middle-aged man, but with a fine soldierly bearing, which took off from his years; and he was so eager to see to the safe exit of his wife from the carriage-door that he had not time to do more than take off his hat to blooming Bella on the steps.

"Now, my love," he exclaimed as the lady's form appeared, "pray take care; two steps: that's right — here you are, safe."

And then Mrs. Damer, being securely landed, was permitted to fly into the cousinly arms which were opened to receive her.

"My dear Bella!"

"My dearest Blanche — I am so delighted to see you again. Why, you are positively frozen! Pray come in at once to the fire. Colonel Damer, my servants will see to the luggage — do leave it to them, and come and warm yourselves."

A couple of men-servants now came forward and offered to see to the unloading of the carriage — but Mrs. Damer did not move.

"Will you not go in, my love, as your cousin proposes?" said her husband. "I can see to the boxes if you should wish me to do so."

"No, thank you," was the low reply; and there was such a ring of melancholy in the voice of Mrs. Damer that a stranger would have been attracted by it. "I prefer waiting until the carriage is unpacked."

"Never mind the luggage, Blanche," whispered Mrs. Clayton, in her coaxing manner. "Come in to the fire, dear — I have so much to tell you."

"Wait a minute, Bella," said her cousin; and the entreaty was so firm that it met with no further opposition.

"One — two — three — four," exclaimed Colonel Damer, as the boxes successively came to the ground. "I am afraid you will think we are going to take you by storm, Mrs. Clayton; but perhaps you know my wife's fancy for a large travelling *kit* of old. Is that all, Blanche?"

"That is all — thank you," in the same low melancholy tones in which she had spoken before. "Now, Bella, dear, which is to be my room?"

"You would rather go there first, Blanche?"

"Yes, please — I'm tired. Will you carry up that box for me?" she continued, pointing out one of the trunks to the servant.

"Directly, ma'am," he returned, as he was looking for change for a sovereign wherewith to accommodate Colonel Damer — but the lady lingered until he was at leisure. Then he shouldered the box next to the one she had indicated, and she directed his attention to the fact, and made him change his burden.

"They'll all go up in time, ma'am," the man remarked; but Mrs. Damer, answering nothing, did not set her foot upon the stairs until he was halfway up them, with the trunk she had desired him to take first.

Then she leaned wearily upon Bella Clayton's arm, pressing it fondly to her side, and so the two went together to the bedroom which had been appointed for the reception of the new guests. It was a large and cosily-furnished apartment, with a dressing-room opening from it. When the ladies arrived there they found the servant awaiting them with the box in question.

"Where will you have it placed, ma'am?" he demanded of Mrs. Damer.

"Under the bed, please."

But the bedstead was a French one, and the mahogany sides were so deep that nothing could get beneath them but dust; and the trunk, although small, was heavy and strong and clamped with iron, not at all the sort of trunk that would go *anywhere*.

"Nothing will go under the bed, ma'am!" said the servant in reply.

Mrs. Damer slightly changed colour.

"Never mind then: leave it there. Oh! what a comfort a good fire is," she continued, turning to the hearth-rug, and throwing herself into an arm-chair. "We have had such a cold drive from the station."

"But about your box, Blanche?" said Mrs. Clayton, who had no idea of her friends being put to any inconvenience. "It can't stand there; you'll unpack it, won't you? or shall I have it moved into the passage?"

"Oh, no, thank you, Bella — please let it stand where it is: it will do very well indeed."

"What will do very well?" exclaimed Colonel Damer, who now entered the bedroom, followed by a servant with another trunk.

"Only Blanche's box, Colonel Damer," said Bella Clayton. "She doesn't wish to unpack it, and it will be in her way here, I'm afraid. It *might* stand in your dressing-room." — This she said as a "feeler," knowing that some gentlemen do not like to be inconvenienced, even in their dressing-rooms.

But Colonel Damer was as unselfish as it was possible for an old Indian to be.

"Of course it can," he replied. "Here (to the servant), just shoulder that box, will you, and move it into the next room."

The man took up the article in question rather carelessly, and nearly let it fall again. Mrs. Damer darted forward as if to save it.

"Pray put it down," she said, nervously. "I have no wish to have it moved — I shall require it by-and-by; it will be no inconvenience — "

"Just as you like, dear," said Mrs. Clayton, who was becoming rather tired of the little discussion. "And now take off your things, dear Blanche, and let me ring for some tea."

Colonel Damer walked into his dressing-room and left the two ladies alone. The remainder of the luggage was brought upstairs; the tea was ordered and served, and whilst Mrs. Clayton busied herself in pouring it out, Mrs. Damer sank back upon a sofa which stood by the fire, and conversed with her cousin.

She had been beautiful, this woman, in her earlier youth, though no one would have thought it to see her now. As Bella handed her the tea she glanced towards the thin hand stretched out to receive it, and from thence to the worn face and hollow eyes, and could scarcely believe she saw the same person she had parted from three years before.

But she had not been so intimate with her of late, and she was almost afraid of commenting upon her cousin's altered appearance, for fear it might wound her; all she said was:

"You look very delicate still, dear Blanche; I was in hopes the change to the Continent would have set you up and made you stronger than you were when you left England."

"Oh, no; I never shall be well again," was Mrs. Damer's careless reply: "it's an old story now, Bella, and it's no use talking about it. Whom have you staying in the house at present, dear?"

"Well, we are nearly full," rejoined Mrs. Clayton. "There is my old godfather, General Knox — you remember him, I know — and his son and daughter; and the Ainsleys and their family; ditto, the Bayleys and the Armstrongs, and then, for single men, we have young Brooke, and Harry's old friend, Charley Moss, and Herbert Laurence, and — are you ill, Blanchey?"

An exclamation had burst from Mrs. Damer — hardly an exclamation, so much as a half-smothered cry — but whether of pain or fear, it was hard to determine.

"Are you ill?" reiterated Mrs. Clayton, full of anxiety for her fragile-looking cousin.

"No," replied Blanche Damer, pressing her hand to her side, but still deadly pale from the effect of whatever emotion she had gone through; "it is nothing; I feel faint after our long journey."

Colonel Damer had also heard the sound, and now appeared upon the threshold of his dressing-room. He was one of those well-meaning, but fussy men, who can never have two women alone for a quarter of an hour without intruding on their privacy.

"Did you call, my dearest?" he asked of his

wife. "Do you want anything?"

"Nothing, thank you," replied Bella for her cousin; "Blanche is only a little tired and overcome by her travelling."

"I think, after all, that I will move that trunk away for you into my room," he said, advancing towards the box which had already been the subject of discussion. Mrs. Damer started from the sofa with a face of crimson.

"I *beg* you will leave my boxes alone," she said, with an imploring tone in her voice which was quite unfitted to the occasion. "I have not brought one more than I need, and I wish them to remain under my own eye."

"There must be something very valuable in that receptacle," said Colonel Damer, facetiously, as he beat a retreat to his own quarters.

"Is it your linen box?" demanded Mrs. Clayton of her cousin.

"Yes," in a hesitating manner; "that is, it contains several things that I have in daily use; but go on about your visitors, Bella: are there any more?"

"I don't think so: where had I got to? — oh! to the bachelors: well, there are Mr. Brooke and Captain Moss, and Mr. Laurence (the poet, you know; Harry was introduced to him last season by Captain Moss), and my brother Alfred; and that's all."

"A very respectable list," said Mrs. Damer, languidly. "What kind of a man is the — the poet you spoke of?"

"Laurence? — oh, he seems a very pleasant man; but he is very silent and abstracted, as I suppose a poet should be. My sister Carrie is here, and they have quite got up a flirtation together; however, I don't suppose it will come to anything."

"And your nursery department?"

"Thriving, thank you; I think you *will* be astonished to see my boy. Old Mrs. Clayton says he is twice the size that Harry was at that age; and the little girls can run about and talk almost as well as I can. But I must not expect you, Blanche, to take the same interest in babies that I do."

This she added, remembering that the woman before her was childless. Mrs. Damer moved uneasily on her couch, but she said nothing; and soon after the sound of a gong reverberating through the hall warned Mrs. Clayton that the dinner was not far off and the riding-party must have returned; so, leaving her friend to her toilet, she took her departure.

As she left the room, Mrs. Damer was alone. She had no maid of her own, and she had refused the offices of Mrs. Clayton, assuring her that she was used to dress herself; but she made little progress in that department, as she lay on the couch in the firelight, with her face buried in her hands, and thoughts coursing through her mind of which heaven alone knew the tendency.

"Come, my darling," said the kind, coaxing voice of her husband, as, after knocking more than once without receiving any answer, he entered her room, fully dressed, and found her still arrayed in her travelling things, and none of her boxes unpacked. "You will never be ready for dinner at this rate. Shall I make an excuse for your not appearing at table this evening? I am sure Mrs. Clayton would wish you to keep your room if you are too tired to dress."

"I am not too tired, Harry," said Mrs. Damer, rising from the couch, "and I shall be ready in ten minutes," unlocking and turning over the contents of a box as she spoke.

"Better not, perhaps, my love," interposed the colonel, in mild expostulation; "you will be better in bed, and can see your kind friends to-morrow morning."

"I am going down to dinner to-night," she answered, gently, but decisively. She was a graceful woman now she stood on her feet, and threw off the heavy wraps in which she had travelled, with a slight, willowy figure, and a complexion which was almost transparent in its delicacy; but her face was very thin, and her large blue eyes had a scared and haggard look in them, which was scarcely less painful to witness than the appearance of anxiety which was expressed by the knitted brows by which they were surmounted. As she now raised her fair attenuated hands to rearrange her hair, which had once been abundant and glossy, her husband could not avoid remarking upon the change which had passed over it.

"I had no idea you had lost your hair so much, darling," he said; "I have not seen it down before to-night. Why, where is it all gone to?" he continued, as he lifted the light mass in his hands, and remembered of what a length and weight it used to be, when he last parted from her.

"Oh, I don't know," she rejoined, sadly; "gone, with my youth, I suppose, Henry."

"My poor girl!" he said, gently, "you have suffered very much in this separation. I had no right to leave you alone for so many years. But it is all over now, dearest, and I will take such good care of you that you will be obliged to get well and strong again."

She turned round suddenly from the glass, and pressed her lips upon the hand which held her hair.

"Don't," she murmured; "pray don't speak to me so, Henry! I can't bear it; I can't indeed!"

He thought it was from excess of feeling that she spoke; and so it was, though not as he imagined. So he changed the subject lightly, and bade her be lazy no longer, but put on her dress, if she was really determined to make one of the party at dinner that evening.

In another minute, Mrs. Damer had brushed her diminished hair into the fashion in which she ordinarily wore it; thrown on an evening-robe of black, which, while it contrasted well with her fairness, showed the falling away of her figure in a painful degree; and was ready to accompany her husband downstairs.

They were met at the door of the drawing-room by their host, who was eager to show cordiality towards guests of whom his wife thought so much, and having also been acquainted himself with Mrs. Damer since her return to England. He led her up to the sofa whereon Bella sat; and, dinner being almost immediately announced, the little hostess was busy pairing off her couples.

"Mr. Laurence!" she exclaimed; and then looking around the room, "where *is* Mr. Laurence?" So that that gentleman was forced to leave the window-curtains, behind which he had ensconced himself, and advance into the centre of the room. "Oh, here you are at last; will you take Mrs. Damer down to dinner?" and proceeding immediately with the usual form of introduction — "Mr. Laurence — Mrs. Damer."

They bowed to each other; but over the lady's face, as she went through her share of the introduction, there passed so indescribable, and yet so unmistakable a change, that Mrs. Clayton, although not very quick, could not help observing it, and she said, involuntarily —

"Have you met Mr. Laurence before, Blanche?"

"I believe I have had that pleasure — in London — many years ago."

The last words came out so faintly that they were almost undistinguishable.

"Why didn't you tell me so?" said Bella Clayton, reproachfully, to Mr. Laurence.

He was beginning to stammer out some excuse about its having been so long ago, when Mrs. Damer came to his aid, in her clear, cold voice —

"It *was* very long ago: we must both be forgiven for having forgotten the circumstance."

"Well, you must renew your acquaintanceship at dinner," said Mrs. Clayton, blithely, as she trotted off to make matters pleasant between the rest of her visitors. As she did so, Mr. Laurence remained standing by the sofa, but he did not attempt to address Mrs. Damer. Only, when the room was nearly cleared, he held out his arm to her, and she rose to accept it. But the next minute she had sunk back again upon the sofa, and Mrs. Clayton was at her cousin's side. Mrs. Damer had fainted.

"Poor darling!" exclaimed Colonel Damer, as he pressed forward to the side of his wife. "I was afraid coming down to-night would be too much for her, but she would make the attempt; she has so much spirit. Pray don't delay the dinner, Mrs. Clayton; I will stay by her, if you will excuse the apparent rudeness, until she is sufficiently recovered to go to bed."

But even as he spoke his wife raised herself from the many arms which supported her, and essayed to gain her feet.

"Bella, dear! I am all right again. Pray, if you love me, don't make a scene about a little fatigue. I often faint now: let me go up to my bedroom and lie down, as I ought to have done at first, and I shall be quite well to-morrow morning."

She would accept no one's help — not even her husband's, though it distressed him greatly that she refused it — but walked out of the room of her own accord, and toiled wearily up the staircase which led her to the higher stories; whilst more than one pair of eyes watched her ascent, and more than one appetite was spoilt for the coming meal.

"Don't you think that Blanche is looking very ill?" demanded Bella Clayton of Colonel Damer, at the dinner-table. She had been much struck herself with the great alteration in her cousin's looks, and fancied that her husband was not so alarmed about it as he ought to be.

"I do, indeed," he replied; "but it is the last thing she will acknowledge herself. She has very bad spirits and appetite; appears always in a low fever, and is so nervous that the least thing will frighten her. That, to me, is the worst and most surprising change of all: such a high-couraged creature as she used to be."

"Yes, indeed," replied Mrs. Clayton; "I can hardly imagine Blanche being nervous at anything. It must have come on since her visit to the Continent, for she was not so when she stayed here last."

"When was that?" demanded the Colonel, anxiously.

"Just three years ago this Christmas," was the answer. "I don't think I ever saw her look better than she did then, and she was the life of the house. But soon afterwards she went to Paris, and then we heard of her illness, and this is my first meeting with her since that time. I was very much shocked when she got out of the carriage: I should scarcely have known her again." Here Mrs. Clayton stopped, seeing that the attention of Mr. Laurence, who sat opposite to her, appeared to be riveted on her words, and Colonel Damer relapsed into thought and spoke no more.

In the meanwhile Mrs. Damer had gained her bedroom. Women had come to attend upon her, sent by their mistress, and laden with offers of refreshment and help of every kind, but she had dismissed them and chosen to be alone. She felt too weak to be very restless, but she had sat by the fire and cried, until she was so exhausted that her bed suggested itself to her, as the best place in which she could be; but rising to undress, preparatory to seeking it, she had nearly fallen, and catching feebly at the bedpost had missed it, and sunk down by the side of the solid black box, which was clamped with iron and fastened with a padlock, and respecting which she had been so particular a few hours before. She felt as if she was dying, and as if this were the fittest place for her to die on. "There is nothing in my possession," she cried, "that really belongs to me but *this* — this which I loathe and abhor, and love and weep over at one and the same moment." And, strange to relate, Mrs. Damer turned on her side and kneeling by the iron-clamped chest pressed her lips upon its hard, unyielding surface, as if it had life wherewith to answer her embrace. And then the wearied creature dragged herself up again into an unsteady position, and managed to sustain it until she was ready to lie down upon her bed.

The next morning she was much better. Colonel Damer and Bella Clayton laid their heads together and decided that she was to remain in bed until after breakfast, therefore she was spared meeting with the assembled strangers until the dinner-hour again, for luncheon was a desultory meal at Molton Chase, and scarcely any of the gentlemen were present at it that day. After luncheon Mrs. Clayton proposed driving Mrs. Damer out in her pony-chaise.

"I don't think you will find it cold, dear, and we can come home by the lower shrubberies and meet the gentlemen as they return from shooting," Colonel Damer being one of the shooting party. But Mrs. Damer had declined the drive, and made her cousin understand so plainly that she preferred being left alone, that Mrs. Clayton felt no compunction in acceding to her wishes, and laying herself out to please the other ladies staying in the house.

And Mrs. Damer did wish to be alone. She wanted to think over the incidents of the night before, and devise some plan by which she could persuade her husband to leave the Grange as soon as possible without provoking questions which she might find it difficult to answer. When the sound of the wheels of her cousin's pony-chaise had died away, and the great stillness pervading Molton Grange proclaimed that she was the sole inmate left behind, she dressed herself in a warm cloak, and drawing the hood over her head prepared for a stroll about the grounds. A little walk she thought would do her good, and with this intention she left the house. The Grange gardens were extensive and curiously laid out, and there were many winding shrubbery paths about them, which strangers were apt to find easier to enter than to find their way out of again. Into one of these Mrs. Damer now turned her steps for the sake of privacy and shelter; but she had not gone far before, on turning an abrupt corner, she came suddenly upon the figure of the gentleman she had been introduced to the night before, Mr. Laurence, who she had imagined to be with the shooting party. He was half lying, half sitting across a rustic seat which encircled the huge trunk of an old tree, with his eyes bent upon the ground and a cigar between his lips. He was more an intellectual and fine-looking than a handsome man, but he possessed two gifts which are much more winning than beauty, a mind of great power, and the art of fascination. As Mrs. Damer came full in view of him, too suddenly to stop herself or to retreat, he rose quickly from the attitude he had assumed when he thought himself secure from interruption and stood in her pathway. She attempted to pass him with an inclination of the head, but he put out his hand and stopped her.

"Blanche! you must speak to me; you shall not pass like this; I insist upon it!" and she tried in vain to disengage her arm from his detaining clasp.

"Mr. Laurence, what right have you to hold me

thus?"

"What right, Blanche? The right of every man over the woman who loves him!"

"That is your right over me no longer. I have tried to avoid you. You have both seen and known it! No *gentleman* would force himself upon my notice in this manner."

"Your taunt fails to have any effect upon me. I have sought an explanation of your extraordinary conduct from you in vain. My letters have been unanswered, my entreaties for a last interview disregarded; and now that chance has brought us together again, I must have what I have a right to ask from your own lips. I did not devise this meeting; I did not even know you had returned to England till yesterday, and then I sought to avoid you; but it was fated that we should meet, and it is fated that you satisfy my curiosity."

"What do you want to know?" she asked, in a low voice.

"First, have you ceased to love me?"

The angry light which had flashed across her face when he used force to detain her died away; the pallid lips commenced to tremble, and in the sunken eyes large tear-drops rose and hung quivering upon the long eyelashes.

"Enough, Blanche," Mr. Laurence continued, in a softer voice. "Nature answers me. I will not give you the needless pain of speaking. Then, why did you forsake me? Why did you leave England without one line of farewell, and why have you refused to hold any communication with me since that time?"

"I *could* not," she murmured. "You do not know; you cannot feel; you could never understand my feelings on that occasion."

"That is no answer to my question, Blanche," he said firmly, "and an answer I will have. What was the immediate cause of your breaking faith with me? I loved you, you know how well. What drove you from me? Was it fear, or indifference, or a sudden remorse?"

"It was," she commenced slowly, and then as if gathering up a great resolution, she suddenly exclaimed, "Do you *really* wish to know what parted us?"

"I really intend to know," he replied, and the old power which he had held over her recommenced its sway. "Whatever it was it has not tended to your happiness," he continued, "if I may judge from your looks. You are terribly changed, Blanche! I think even I could have made you happier than you appear to have been."

"I have had enough to change me," she replied. "If you will know then, come with me, and I will show you."

"To-day?"

"At once; to-morrow may be too late." She began to walk towards the house as she spoke, rapidly and irregularly, her heart beating fast, but no trace of weakness in her limbs; and Herbert Laurence followed her, he scarcely knew why, expecting that she had desired it.

Into Molton Grange she went, up the broad staircase and to her chamber door before she paused to see if he was following. When she did so she found that he stood just behind her on the wide landing.

"You can enter," she said, throwing open the door of her bedroom, "don't be afraid; there is nothing here except the cause for which I parted with you." In her agitation and excitement, scarcely pausing to fasten the door behind her, Mrs. Damer fell down on her knees before the little black box with its iron clamps and ponderous padlock; and drawing a key from her bosom, applied it to the lock, and in another minute had thrown back the heavy lid. Having displaced some linen which lay at the top, she carefully removed some lighter materials, and then calling to the man behind her, bid him look in and be satisfied. Mr. Laurence advanced to the box, quite ignorant as to the reason of her demand; but as his eye fell upon its contents, he started backwards and covered his face with his hands. As he drew them slowly away again he met the sad, earnest look with which the kneeling woman greeted him, and for a few moments they gazed at one another in complete silence. Then Mrs. Damer withdrew her eyes from his and rearranged the contents of the black box; the heavy lid shut with a clang, the padlock was fast again, the key in her bosom, and she rose to her feet and prepared to leave the room in the same unbroken silence. But he again detained her, and this time his voice was hoarse and changed.

"Blanche! tell me, is this the truth?"

"As I believe in heaven," she answered.

"And this was the reason that we parted — this the sole cause of our estrangement?"

"Was it not enough?" she said. "I erred, but it

was as one in a dream. When I awoke I could no longer err and be at peace. At peace did I say? I have known no peace since I knew you; but I should have died and waked up in hell, if I had not parted with you. This is all the truth, believe it or not as you will; but there may, there can be nothing in future between you and me. Pray let me pass you."

"But that — that — box, Blanche!" exclaimed Herbert Laurence, with drops of sweat, notwithstanding the temperature of the day, upon his forehead. "It was an accident, a misfortune; *you* did not do it?"

She turned upon him eyes which were full of mingled horror and scorn.

"I *do* it!" she said; "what are you dreaming of? I was mad; but not so mad as that! How could you think it?" and the tears rose in her eyes more at the supposition which his question had raised than at the idea that he could so misjudge her.

"But why do you keep this? why do you carry it about with you, Blanche? It is pure insanity on your part. How long is it since you have travelled in company with that dreadful box?"

"More than two years," she said in a fearful whisper. "I have tried to get rid of it, but to no purpose; there was always some one in the way. I have reasoned with myself, and prayed to be delivered from it, but I have never found an opportunity. And now, what does it matter? The burden and heat of the day are past."

"Let me do it for you," said Mr. Laurence. "Whatever our future relation to one another, I cannot consent that you should run so terrible a risk through fault of mine. The strain upon your mind has been too great already. Would to heaven I could have borne it for you! but you forbid me even the privilege of knowing that you suffered. Now that I have ascertained it, it must be my care that the cause of our separation shall at least live in your memory only." And as he finished speaking he attempted to lift the box; but Mrs. Damer sprang forward and prevented him.

"Leave it!" she cried; "do not dare to touch it; it is *mine*! It has gone wherever I have gone for years. Do you think, for the little space that is left me, that I would part with the only link left between me and my dread past?" and saying this she threw herself upon the black trunk and burst into tears.

"Blanche! you love me as you ever did," exclaimed Herbert Laurence. "These tears confess it. Let me make amends to you for this; let me try to make the happiness of your future life!"

But before his sentence was concluded Mrs. Damer had risen from her drooping attitude and stood before him.

"Make amends!" she echoed scornfully. "How can you 'make amends'? Nothing can wipe out the memory of the shame and misery that I have passed through, nothing restore the quiet conscience I have lost. I do not know if I love you still or not. When I think of it, my head swims, and I only feel confused and anxious. But I am sure of one thing, that the horror of my remorse for even having listened to you has power to overwhelm any regret that may be lingering in my unworthy breast, and that the mere fact of your bodily presence is agony to me. When I met you to-day I was battling with my invention to devise some means of leaving the place where you are without exciting suspicion. If you ever loved, have pity on me now; take the initiative, and rid me of yourself."

"Is this your final decision, Blanche?" he asked, slowly. "Will you not regret it when too late, and you are left alone with only *that*?"

She shuddered, and he caught at the fact as a sign of relenting.

"Dearest, loveliest," he commenced. — This woman had been the loveliest to him in days gone past, and though she was so terribly changed in eyes that regarded her less, Herbert Laurence, her once lover, could still trace above the languor and debility and distress of her present appearance, the fresh, sparkling woman who had sacrificed herself for his sake; and although his style of address signified more than he really thought for her, the knowledge of how much she had undergone since their separation had the power to make him imagine that this partial reanimation of an old flame was a proof that the fire which kindled it had never perished. Therefore it did not appear absurd in his mental eyes to preface his appeal to Mrs. Damer thus: "Dearest, loveliest — " but she turned upon him as though he had insulted her.

"Mr. Laurence!" she exclaimed, "I have told you that the past is past; be good enough to take me at my word. Do you think that I have lived over two years of solitary shame and grief, to break the heart that trusts in me *now*? If I had any wish, or any thought to the contrary, it would be impossible. I am enveloped by kind words and acts, by care and attention, which chain me as closely to my home as if I were kept a prisoner between four walls. I could not free myself if I would," she continued, throwing back her arms, as though she tried to break an invisible thrall. "I must die first; the cords of gratitude are bound about me so closely. It is killing me, as nothing else could kill," she added, in a lower voice. "I lived under your loss, and the knowledge of my own disgrace; but I cannot live under his perpetual kindness and perfect trust. It cannot last much longer: for mercy's sake, leave me in peace until the end comes!"

"And the box?" he demanded.

"I will provide for the box before that time," she answered, sadly; "but if you have any fear, keep the key yourself: the lock is not one that can be forced."

She took the key from her bosom, where it hung on a broad black ribbon, as she spoke, and handed it to him. He accepted it without demur.

"You are so rash," he said; "it will be safer with me: let me take the box also?"

"No, no!" said Mrs. Damer, hurriedly; "you shall not; and it would be no use. If it were out of my sight, I should dream that it was found, and talk of it in my sleep. I often rise in the night now to see if it is safe. Nothing could do away with it. If you buried it, some one would dig it up; if you threw it in the water, it would float. It would lie still nowhere but on my heart, where it ought to be! — it ought to be!"

Her eyes had reassumed the wild, restless expression which they took whilst speaking of the past, and her voice had sunk to a low, fearful whisper.

"This is madness," muttered Herbert Laurence; and he was right. On the subject of the black box Mrs. Damer's brain was turned.

He was just about to speak to her again, and try to reason her out of her folly, when voices were heard merrily talking together in the hall, and her face worked with the dread of discovery.

"Go!" she said; "pray, go at once. I have told you everything." And in another moment Herbert Laurence had dashed through the passage to the privacy of his own room; and Mrs. Clayton, glowing from her drive, and with a fine rosy baby in her arms, had entered the apartment of her cousin.

II

Bella found her cousin sitting in an arm-chair, with the cloak still over her shoulders, and a face of ashy whiteness, the reaction of her excitement.

"My dear, how ill you look!" was her first exclamation. "Have you been out?"

"I went a little way into the shrubberies," said Mrs. Damer; "but the day turned so cold."

"Do you think so? We have all been saying what a genial afternoon it is: but it certainly does not seem to have agreed with you. Look at my boy: isn't he a fine fellow? — he has been out all day in the garden. I often wish you had a child, Blanchey."

"Do you, dear? it is more than I do."

"Ah, but you can't tell, till they are really yours, how much pleasure they give you; no one knows who has not been a mother."

"No; I suppose not."

Mrs. Damer shivered as she said the words, and looked into the baby's fat, unmeaning face with eyes of sad import. Mrs. Clayton thought she had wounded her cousin, and stooped to kiss the slight offence away; but she fancied that Blanche almost shrunk from her embrace.

"She must be really ill," thought the kindly little Bella, who had no notion of such a thing as heart-sickness for an apparently happy married woman. "She ought to see a doctor: I shall tell Colonel Damer so."

In another half-hour they were at her side together, urging her to take their advice.

"Now, my darling," said the Colonel, when Mrs. Damer faintly protested against being made a fuss about, "you must be good for my sake. You know how precious you are to me, and how it would grieve me to have you laid up; let me send for Dr. Barlow, as your cousin advises. You were very much overcome by the long journey here, and I am afraid the subsequent excitement of seeing your kind friends has been too much for you. You do not half know how dear you are to me, Blanche, or you would not refuse such a trifling request. Here have I been, for five years, dearest, only looking forward from day to day to meeting my dear loving little wife again; and then to have you so ill as this the first month of our reunion, is a great trial to me. Pray let me send for Dr. Barlow."

But Mrs. Damer pleaded for delay. She had become chilled through being out in the shrubberies; she had not yet got over the fatigue of her journey; she had caught a cold whilst crossing from Havre to Folkestone: it was anything and everything but an illness which required medical attendance. If she were not better in the morning, she promised to make no opposition to their wishes.

So she forced herself to rise and dress for dinner. She appeared there calm and collected, and continued so throughout the evening, talking with Mr. Laurence quite as much as with the rest of the company; and she went to bed at the same hour as the other guests of Molton Grange, receiving with her cousin's good-night, congratulations on the evident improvement of her health.

"I cannot quite make out what has come to that cousin of yours, Bella," said Harry Clayton to his wife, as they too retired for the night; "she doesn't appear half such a jolly woman as she used to be."

"She is certainly very much altered," was Mrs. Clayton's response; "but I think it must be chiefly owing to her health; a feeling of debility is so very depressing."

"I suppose it can't be anything on her mind, Bella?" suggested the husband, after a pause.

"On her *mind*, Harry!" said Bella, sitting up in bed in her wonderment; "of course not; why, how could it be? She has everything she can wish for; and, I am sure, no woman could have a more devoted husband than Colonel Damer. He has been speaking a great deal about her to me to-day, and his anxiety is something enormous. On her *mind*! — what a funny idea, Harry; what could have put that in your head?"

"I am sure I don't know," was the husband's reply, rather ruefully given, as if conscious he had made a great mistake.

"You old *goose*," said his wife, with an emphatic kiss, as she composed herself to her innocent slumbers.

But before they were broken by nature, in the gray of the morning, Mrs. Clayton was roused by a tapping at the bedroom door; a tapping to which all Mr. Clayton's shouts to "come in," only served as a renewal.

"Who can it be, Harry? — do get up and see," said Bella.

So Harry got up, like a dutiful husband, and opened the door, and the figure of Colonel Damer, robed in a dressing-gown, and looking very shadowy and unreal in the dawning, presented itself on the threshold.

"Is your wife here?" demanded the Colonel briefly.

"Of course she is," said Mr. Clayton, wondering what the Colonel wanted with her.

"Will she come to Mrs. Damer? she is *very* ill," was the next sentence, delivered tremblingly.

"Very ill!" exclaimed Bella, jumping out of bed and wrapping herself in a dressing-gown. "How do you mean, Colonel Damer? — when did it happen?"

"God knows!" he said, in an agitated voice; "but for some time after she fell asleep she was feverish and excited, and spoke much. I woke suddenly in the night and missed her, and going in search of her with a light, found her fallen on the landing."

"Fainted?" said Bella.

"I don't know now whether it was a faint or a fit," he replied, "but I incline to the latter belief. I carried her back to her bed, and gave her some restoratives, not liking to disturb you — "

"Oh! why didn't you, Colonel Damer?" interposed his hostess.

" — and thought she was better, till just now, when she had another attack of unconsciousness, and is so weak after it she cannot move. She has fever too, I am sure, from the rapidity of her pulse, and I don't think her head is quite clear."

"Harry, dear, send for Dr. Barlow at once," thrusting her naked feet into slippers, "and come back with me, Colonel Damer; she should not be left for a minute."

And she passed swiftly along the corridor to her cousin's room. As she neared that of Mr. Laurence, the door opened a little, and a voice asked huskily —

"Is anything the matter, Mrs. Clayton? I have been listening to noises in the house for the last hour."

"My cousin, Mrs. Damer, has been taken ill, Mr. Laurence, but we have sent for the doctor; I am going to her now."

And as the door closed again she fancied that she heard a sigh.

Blanche Damer was lying on her pillows very hot and flushed, with that anxious, perturbed look which the eyes assume when the brain is only half clouded, and can feel itself to be wandering.

"Blanche, dearest," cried Bella, as she caught sight of her face, "what is the matter? How did this happen?"

"I dreamt that he had taken it," said Mrs. Damer, slowly and sadly; "but it was a mistake: he must not have it yet — not yet! only a little while to wait now! — but he has the key."

"Her mind is wandering at present," said Colonel Damer, who had followed Mrs. Clayton into the room.

"Oh, Colonel Damer," exclaimed Bella, tearfully, "how dreadful it is! — she frightens me! Could she have knocked her head in falling? Have you no idea why she got up and went into the passage?"

"Not the slightest," he returned. And now that she examined him under the morning light, which was by this time streaming through the open shutters, Bella Clayton saw how aged and haggard his night's anxiety had made him look. "My wife has been very subject to both sleeping-talking and walking since my return, and I have several times missed her, as I did last night, and found her walking about the room in her sleep, but she has never been like this before. When I first found her in the passage, I asked her why she had gone there, or what she wanted, and she said, 'the key.' When I had relifted her into bed, I found her bunch of keys as usual, on the dressing-table, therefore I imagine she could not then have known what she was talking about. I trust Dr. Barlow will not be long in coming; I am deeply anxious."

And he looked the truth of what he uttered; whilst poor little Mrs. Clayton could only press his hand and entreat him to be hopeful; and his wife lay on her pillows, and silently stared into vacancy.

As soon as the doctor arrived he pronounced the patient to be suffering from an attack of pressure on the brain, and wished to know whether she had not been subjected to some great mental shock or strain.

Here Colonel Damer came forward and stoutly denied the possibility of such a thing. He had joined his wife from India a month ago, at which time she was, though in delicate, not in bad health, and he had never left her since. They had crossed from Havre to Folkestone three days before, and Mrs. Damer had not complained of any unusual sickness or fatigue. She was a person of a highly excitable and nervous temperament, and her appetite and spirit were variable; otherwise there had been nothing in her state of health to call for anxiety on the part of her friends.

Dr. Barlow listened to all these statements, and believed as much of them as he chose. However he waived the subject of the cause of the disaster; the fact that it had occurred was undeniable; and the remedies for such emergencies were immediately resorted to. But all proved alike ineffectual, for the simple reason that the irrevocable fiat had gone forth, and Blanche Damer was appointed to die.

As the day wore on, and the case assumed a darker aspect, and the doctor's prognostications became less hopeful, Colonel Damer worked himself into a perfect frenzy of fear.

"Save her, Dr. Barlow," he had said to that gentleman, in the insane manner in which people are used to address the Faculty, as if it was in their power to do more than help the efforts of nature. "Save her life, for God's sake! and there is nothing that I can do for you, of earthly good, that shall not be yours. Shall I call in other advice? Shall I telegraph to London? Is there anyone there who can save her? It is my life as well as hers that is trembling in the scale. For the love of heaven, do not stand on ceremony, but only tell me what is best to be done!"

Of course Dr. Barlow told him that if he was not perfectly satisfied, he should wish him to telegraph to town for further advice, and mentioned several names celebrated in such cases; at the same time he assured Colonel Damer that he did not believe any number of doctors could do more for the patient than he was doing, and that it was impossible to guess at the probable termination of the illness for some days to come.

Bella Clayton gave up the duty of amusing her guests, and stationed herself at the bedside of her cousin; and the unhappy husband wandered in and out of the room like a ghost; trying to think upon each fresh visit, that there was a slight improvement in the symptoms, and spending the intervening time in praying for the life which he fondly imagined had been devoted to himself. Meanwhile, whenever Mrs. Damer opened her lips, it was to ramble on in this manner:

"Dying!" her hollow voice would exclaim; "crushed to death beneath the weight of a pyramid of blessings that lies like lead upon my chest and reaches to the ceiling. Kind words — fond care, and sweet attentions — they bow me down to the earth! I am stifling beneath the burden of their silent reproaches. Two and two are four; and four and four is eight; eight times locked should be secure — but there is a worm that dieth not, and a fire that is not quenched."

"Oh! don't come in here, Colonel Damer," poor Bella would exclaim, as the unhappy man would creep to the foot of the bed and stand listening, with blanched cheeks, to the delirious ravings of his wife. "She doesn't know what she is saying, remember;

and she will be better to-morrow, doubtless. Don't distress yourself more, by listening to all this nonsense."

"I don't believe she will ever be better, Mrs. Clayton," he replied, on one of these occasions. This was on the third day.

"Dearest!" the sick woman resumed, in a plaintively soft voice, without being in the least disturbed by the conversation around her, "if you have ever loved me, you will believe in this hour that I love you in return. If you have given me your love, I have given you more than my life."

"Does she speak of me?" demanded Colonel Damer.

"I think so," said Bella Clayton, sadly.

"Take it off! take it off!" cried Mrs. Damer, starting with terror — "this box — this iron-clamped box which presses on my soul. What have I done? Where shall I go? How am I to meet him again?"

"What does she say?" asked the Colonel, trembling.

"Colonel Damer, I must beg you to quit the room," said Bella, weeping. "I cannot bear to stay here with both of you. Pray leave me alone with Blanche until she is quieter."

And so the husband left the chamber, with fellow tears in his eyes, and she set herself to the painful task of attempting to soothe the delirious woman.

"If he would only strike me," moaned Mrs. Damer, "or frown at me, or tell me that I lie, I could bear it better; but he is killing me with kindness.

Where is the box? — open it — let him see all. I am ready to die. But I forgot — there is no key, and no one shall touch it: it is mine — mine. Hark! I hear it! I hear it! How could I put it there? Let me go — no one shall hold me! Let me go, I say — I *hear* it; and — and — the world is nothing to me!"

At last, when they had almost despaired of ever seeing her sleep again, there came an uninterrupted hour of repose from sheer weariness; and then wide-open hollow eyes — a changed voice sounding with the question — "Bella! have I been ill?" and Mrs. Damer's delirium was over.

Over with her life. For on his next visit Dr. Barlow found her sensible but cold and pulseless, and broke to her friends the news that twelve hours more would end her existence.

Colonel Damer went wild, and telegraphed at once to London for men who arrived when his wife was ready to be coffined. Bella heard the decree and wept silently; and a great gloom fell upon the guests of Molton Chase, who had been left altogether on poor Harry's hands since Mrs. Damer's illness.

The dying woman lay very silent and exhausted for some time after she had waked from that brief, memory-restoring sleep. When she next spoke, she said, observing her cousin's swollen eyes —

"Am I dying, Bella?"

Poor little Mrs. Clayton did not at all know what answer to make to such a direct question, but she managed to stammer out something which, whatever it was meant for, was taken as affirmative by the one it most concerned.

"I thought so. Shall I never be able to get out of bed again?"

"I am afraid not, darling — you are so weak!"

"Yes, I am — I can hardly raise my hand. And yet I must rise if I can. I have something so particular to do."

"Cannot I do it for you, Blanche?"

"*Will* you do it, Bella?"

"Anything — everything, love! How can you ask me?"

"And you will promise secrecy? Let me look in your face. Yes, it is a true face, as it has ever been, and I can trust you. Have the black box moved out of my room before I die, Bella — mind, *before* I die, and placed in your own dressing-room."

"What, dear, your linen box?"

"Yes, my linen box, or whatever you choose to call it. Take it away *at once*, Bella. Tell no one; and when I am dead, have it buried in my grave. Surely you could manage so much for me!"

"And Colonel Damer?"

"If you speak to him about it, Bella, or to your husband, or to any one, I'll never forgive you, and I'm dying!" cried Mrs. Damer, almost rising in her excitement. "Oh! why have I delayed it so long, why did I not see to this before? I cannot even die in peace."

"Yes, yes, dearest Blanche, I will do it, indeed I will," said Mrs. Clayton, alarmed at her emotion; "and no one shall know of it but myself. Shall I send it to my room at once? You may trust entirely to my discretion. Pray, have no fear!"

"Yes! at once — directly; it cannot be too soon!" said Mrs. Damer, falling back exhausted on her pillow. So a servant was called, and the iron-clamped box was carried away from the sick-room and secreted in Mrs. Clayton's private apartment. Mrs. Damer seemed so weak, that her cousin suggested summoning her husband to her side, but she appeared to shrink from an interview with him.

"I have nothing to say but what will make him sad to think of afterwards," she murmured. "Let me die with you alone, dear Bella. It is better so."

So Colonel Damer, although he went backwards and forwards all the night, was not called at any particular moment to see the last of his wife, and Blanche had her wish. She died alone with her faithful little cousin before the morning broke. As she was just going, she said, in a vague sort of manner —

"Tell him, Bella, that I forgive him as I hope to be forgiven. And that I have seen Heaven open to-night, and a child spirit pleading with the Woman-born for us; and that the burden is lifted off my soul at last." And then she added solemnly — "I will arise and go to my Father — ," and went before she could finish the sentence.

Innocent Bella repeated her last message in perfect faith to Colonel Damer.

"She told me to tell you, that she felt herself forgiven, and that she had seen Heaven opened for her, and the weight of her sins was lifted off her soul. Oh! Colonel Damer, pray think of that, and take comfort. She is happier than you could make her."

But the poor faithful husband was, for the present, beyond all reach of comfort.

The London doctors arrived with the daylight, and had to be solemnly entertained at breakfast, and warmed and comforted before they were despatched home again. The Christmas guests were all packing up their boxes, preparatory to taking their leave of Molton Chase, for it was impossible to think of festivities with such a bereavement in the house. And Harry Clayton told his wife that he was very thankful that they thought of doing so.

"It has been a most unfortunate business altogether, Bella, and of course they all felt it, poor things; and the more so because they could take no active part in it. The house has had a pall over it the last week; and it would have been still worse if they had remained. As for Laurence, I never saw a man so cut up. He has eaten nothing since your poor cousin was taken ill. One would think she had been his sister, or his dearest friend."

"Is he going with the rest, Harry?"

"No; he will stay till after the funeral; then he is going abroad. He feels deeply with you, Bella, and desired me to tell you so."

"He is very good — thank him in my name."

*****

But released from the care of thinking for her guests, and sitting crying alone in her dressing-room, poor Mrs. Clayton could not imagine what to do with the iron-clamped black box. She had promised Blanche not to confide in her husband, or Colonel Damer. The latter, having no family vault, wished to lay the remains of his wife amongst those of the Claytons in the country churchyard of Molton; but how to get the black box conveyed to the grave without the knowledge of the chief mourners was a mystery beyond the fathoming of Bella's open heart. But in the midst of her perplexity, Fate sent her aid. On the second day of her cousin's death, a gentle tap sounded at her chamber door, and on her invitation to enter being answered, she was surprised to see Mr. Laurence on the threshold — come, as she imagined, to offer his sympathy in person.

"This is very kind of you, Mr. Laurence," she said.

"I can scarcely claim your gratitude, Mrs. Clayton. I have sought you to speak on a very important but painful subject. May I ask your attention for a few moments?"

"Of course you may!" And she motioned him to a seat.

"It concerns her whom we have lost. Mrs. Clayton, tell me truly — did you love your cousin?"

"Dearly — very dearly, Mr. Laurence. We were brought up together."

"Then I may depend on your discretion; and if you wish to save her memory you must exercise it in her behalf. There is a small iron-clamped black trunk amongst her boxes, which must not fall into Colonel Damer's hands. Will you have that box conveyed from her chamber to your own, and (if you will so far trust my honour) make it over to me?"

"To you, Mr. Laurence — the iron-bound box? What possible knowledge can you have of my cousin's secret?"

"Her secret?"

"Yes — she confided that box to my care the night she died. She made me promise to do (without question) what you have just asked me to perform, and I did it. The trunk is already here."

And throwing open a cupboard at the side of the room, she showed him the chest which he had mentioned.

"I see that it is," he answered. "How do you design disposing of it?"

"She wished it to be buried in her grave."

"That is impossible in its present state. The contents must be removed."

"But how?" Mrs. Clayton demanded, in surprise. "It is locked and double locked, and there is no key."

"*I* have the key," he answered, gravely.

"Oh! Mr. Laurence," exclaimed his hostess, trembling, "there is some dreadful mystery here. For heaven's sake tell me what it is! What connection can you possibly have with this box of my poor cousin's, if you have only met her once in your life?"

"Did she say so?" he asked.

"No; but I fancied so. Have you known her? When? where? and why did you not tell us so before?"

"How can I tell you now?" he said, gazing into the pure womanly face upraised to his own, bearing an expression which was half-surprise and half-fear but which seemed as though it could never dream of anything like shame.

"You are too good and too happy, Mrs. Clayton, to know of, or be able to sympathize with, the troubles and temptations which preceded our fatal friendship and her fall."

"Blanche's *fall!*" ejaculated Bella Clayton, in a voice of horror.

"Don't interrupt me, please, Mrs. Clayton," he said, hurriedly, covering his face with his hands, "or I shall never be able to tell you the wretched story. I knew your cousin years ago. Had you any suspicion that she was unhappy in her marriage?"

"No! none!" replied Bella, with looks of surprise.

"She *was* then, thoroughly unhappy, as scores of women are, simply because the hearts of the men they are bound to are opposed to theirs in every taste and feeling. I met her when she first returned to England, and — it is the old story, Mrs. Clayton — I loved her, and was mad enough to tell her so. When a selfish man and an unselfish woman have mutually confessed their preference for each other, the result is easily anticipated. I ruined her — forgive my plain speaking — and she still loved on, and forgave me."

"Oh, Blanche!" exclaimed Bella Clayton, hiding her hot face in her hands.

"We lived in a fool's paradise for some months, and then one day she left her house and went to the Continent, without giving me any warning of her intention. I was thunderstruck when I heard it, and deeply hurt, and as soon as I had traced her to Paris, I followed and demanded an explanation of her conduct. But she refused to see me, and when she found me pertinacious, left the city as suddenly as she had done that of London. Since which time she has answered no letters of mine, nor did we ever meet until, most unexpectedly, I met her in your house. My pride, after her first refusals to see me, was too great to permit me to renew my entreaties, and so I called her a flirt, and inconstant. I tried to banish her remembrance from my heart — and I thought I had succeeded."

"Oh, my poor darling!" exclaimed Mrs. Clayton. "This accounts then for her holding aloof from all her relations for so long a time, by which means she estranged herself from many of them. She was working out her penitence and deep remorse in solitary misery; and she would not even let me share her confidence. But about the box, Mr. Laurence; what has all this to do with the black box?"

"When I met her in your shrubbery the other day, and reproached her for her desertion of me, insisting upon her giving me the reason of her change of mind, she bade me follow her to her own apartment. There, unlocking the box before you, she showed me its contents."

"And they are — ?" inquired Mrs. Clayton, breathlessly.

"Would you like to see them?" he demanded, taking a key from his pocket. "I have as much right to show them you as she would have had. But is your love for her dead memory and reputation strong enough to insure your eternal secrecy on the subject?"

"It is," said Bella Clayton, decidedly.

"This box," continued Mr. Laurence, applying

the key he held to the lock of the iron-clamped black trunk, "has accompanied my poor girl on all her travels for the last two years. The dreadful secret of its contents which she bore in silent, solitary misery all that time has been, I believe, the ultimate cause of her death, by proving too heavy a burden for the sensitive and proud spirit which was forced to endure the knowledge of its shame. She was killed by her remorse. If you have courage, Mrs. Clayton, for the sight, look at *this* — and pity the feelings I must endure as I kneel here and look at it with you."

He threw back the lid and the topmost linen as he spoke, and Bella Clayton pressed eagerly forward to see, carefully laid amidst withered flowers and folds of cambric, the tiny skeleton of a newborn creature whose angel was even then beholding the face of his Father in Heaven.

She covered her eyes with her clasped hands, no less to shut out the sight than to catch the womanly tears which poured forth at it, and then she cried between her sobs —

"Oh! my poor, poor Blanche, what must she not have suffered! God have mercy on her soul!"

"Amen!" said Herbert Laurence.

"You will let me take the box away with me, Mrs. Clayton?" he asked, gently.

She looked up as he spoke, and the tears were standing in his eyes.

"Yes — yes," she said; "take it away; do what you will with it, only never speak of it to me again."

He never did but once, and that was but an allusion. On the evening of the day on which they committed the remains of Blanche Damer to the dust, he lay in wait for Mrs. Clayton on the landing.

"All has been done as she desired," he whispered; and Mrs. Clayton asked for no further explanation. The secret of which she had been made an unwilling recipient pressed so heavily on her conscience, that she was thankful when he left Molton Grange and went abroad, as he had expressed his intention of doing.

Since which time she has never seen Herbert Laurence again; and Colonel Damer, whose grief at the funeral and for some time after was nearly frenzied, having — like most men who mourn much outwardly — found a source of consolation in the shape of another wife, the story of Blanche Damer's life and death is remembered, for aught her cousin knows to the contrary, by none but herself.

I feel that an objection will be raised to this episode by some people on the score of its being *unnatural*; to whom all I can say in answer is, that the principal incident on which the interest of it turns — that of the unhappy Mrs. Damer having been made so great a coward by conscience that she carried the proof of her frailty about with her for years, too fearful of discovery to permit it to leave her sight — is *a fact*.

To vary the circumstances under which the discovery of the contents of the black box was finally made, and to alter the names of places and people so as to avoid general recognition, I have made my province: to relate the story itself, since, in the form I now present it to my readers, it can give pain to no one, I consider my privilege.

VIII. My Fascinating Friend — William Archer

I

Nature has cursed me with a retiring disposition. I have gone round the world without making a single friend by the way. Coming out of my own shell is as difficult to me as drawing others out of theirs. There are some men who go through life extracting the substance of every one they meet, as one picks out periwinkles with a pin. To me my fellow-men are oysters, and I have no oyster-knife; my sole consolation (if it be one) is that my own values absolutely defy the oyster-knives of others. Not more than twice or thrice in my life have I met a fellow-creature at whose "Open Sesame" the treasures of my heart and brain stood instantly revealed. My Fascinating Friend was one of these rare and sympathetic beings.

I was lounging away a few days at Monaco, awaiting a summons to join some relations in Italy. One afternoon I had started for an aimless and rambling climb among the olive-terraces on the lower slopes of the Tête du Chien. Finding an exquisite coign of vantage amid the roots of a gnarled old trunk springing from a built-up semicircular patch of level ground, I sat me down to rest, and read, and dream. Below me, a little to the right, Monaco jutted out into the purple sea. I could distinguish carriages and pedestrians coming and going on the chaussée between the promontory and Monte Carlo, but I was far too high for any sound to reach me. Away to the left the coast took a magnificent sweep, past the clustering houses of Roccabruna, past the mountains at whose base Mentone nestled unseen, past the Italian frontier, past the bight of Ventimiglia, to where the Capo di Bordighera stood faintly outlined between sea and sky. There was not a solitary sail on the whole expanse of the Mediterranean. A line of white, curving at rhythmic intervals along a small patch of sandy beach, showed that there was a gentle swell upon the sea, but its surface was mirror-like. A lovelier scene there is not in the world, and it was at its very loveliest. I took the *Saturday Review* from my pocket, and was soon immersed in an article on the commutation of tithes.

I was aroused from my absorption by the rattle of a small stone hopping down the steep track, half path, half stairway, by which I had ascended. It had been loosened by the foot of a descending wayfarer, in whom, as he picked his way slowly downward, I recognized a middle-aged German (that I supposed to be his nationality) who had been very assiduous at the roulette-tables of the Casino for some days past. There was nothing remarkable in his appearance, his spectacled eyes, squat nose, and square-cropped bristling beard being simply characteristic of his class and country. He did not notice me as he went by, being too intent on his footing to look about him; but I was so placed that it was a minute or more before he passed out of sight round a bend in the path. He was just turning the corner, and my eyes were still fixed on him, when I was conscious of another figure within my field of vision. This second comer had descended the same pathway, but had loosened no stones on his passage. He trod with such exquisite lightness and agility that he had passed close by me without my being aware of his presence, while he, for his part, had his eyes fixed with a curious intensity on the thick-set figure of the German, upon whom, at his rate of progress, he must have been gaining rapidly. A glance showed me that he was a young man of slender figure, dressed in a suit of dark-coloured tweed, of English cut, and wearing a light-brown wide-awake hat. Just as my eye fell upon him he put his hand into the inner breast-pocket of his coat, and drew from it something which, as he was now well past me, I could not see. At the same moment some small object, probably jerked out of his pocket by mistake, fell almost noiselessly on the path at his feet. In his apparently eager haste he did not notice his loss, but was gliding onward, leaving what I took to be his purse lying on the path. It was clearly my duty to call his attention to it; so I said, "Hi!" an interjection which I have found serves its purpose in all countries. He gave a perceptible start, and looked round at me over his shoulder. I pointed to the object he had dropped, and said, "*Voilà!*" He had thrust back into his pocket the thing, whatever it was, which he held in his hand, and now turned round to look where I was pointing. "Ah!" he said in English, "my cigarette-case! I am much obliged to you," and he stooped and picked it up.

"I thought it was your purse," I said.

"I would rather have lost my purse than this," he said, with a light laugh. He had apparently abandoned his intention of overtaking the German, who had meanwhile passed out of sight.

"Are you such an enthusiastic smoker?" I asked.

"I go in for quality, not quantity," he replied; "and a Spanish friend has just given me some incomparable *cigarritos*." He opened the case as he ascended the few steps which brought him up to my little plateau. "Have one?" he said, holding it out to me with the most winning smile I have ever seen on any human face.

I was about to take one from the left-hand side of the case, when he turned it away and presented the other side to me.

"No, no!" he said; "these flat ones are my common brand. The round ones are the gems."

"I am robbing you," I said, as I took one.

"Not if you are smoker enough to appreciate it," he said, as he stretched himself on the ground beside me, and produced from a little gold matchbox a wax vesta, with which he lighted my cigarette and his own.

So graceful was his whole personality, so easy and charming his manner, that it did not strike me as in the least odd that he should thus make friends with me by the mere exchange of half a dozen words. I looked at him as he lay resting on his elbows and smoking lazily. He had thrown his hat off, and his wavy hair, longish and of an opaque charcoal black, fell over his temples while he shook it back behind his ears. He was a little above the middle height, of dark complexion, with large and soft black eyes and arched eyebrows, a small and rather broad nose (the worst feature in his face), full curving and sensitive lips, and a very strong and rounded chin. He was absolutely beardless, but a slight black down on the upper lip announced a coming mustache. His age could not have been more than twenty. The cut of his clothes, as I have said, was English, but his large black satin neckcloth, flowing out over the collar of his coat, was such as no home-keeping Englishman would ever have dared to appear in. This detail, combined with his accent, perfectly pure but a trifle precise and deliberate, led me to take him for an Englishman brought up on the Continent — probably in Italy, for there was no French intonation in his speech. His voice was rich, but deep — a light baritone.

He took up my *Saturday Review*.

"The Bible of the Englishman abroad," he said. "One of the institutions that makes me proud of our country."

"I have it sent me every week," I said.

"So had my father," he replied. "He used to say, 'Shakespeare we share with the Americans, but damn it, the *Saturday Review* is all our own!' He was one of the old school, my father."

"And the good school," I said, with enthusiasm. "So am I."

"Now, I'm a bit of a Radical," my new friend rejoined, looking up with a smile, which made the confession charming rather than objectionable; and from this point we started upon a discussion, every word of which I could write down if I chose, such a lasting impression did it make upon me. He was indeed a brilliant talker, having read much and travelled enormously for one so young. "I think I have lived in every country in Europe," he said, "except Russia. Somehow it has never interested me." I found that he was a Cambridge man, or, at least, was intimately acquainted with Cambridge life and thought; and this was another bond between us. His Radicalism was not very formidable; it amounted to little more, indeed, than a turn for humorous paradox. Our discussion reminded me of Fuller's description of the wit-combats between Ben Jonson and Shakespeare at the "Mermaid." I was the Spanish galleon, my Fascinating Friend was the English man-of-war, ready "to take advantage of all winds by the quickness of his wit and invention." An hour sped away delightfully, the only thing I did not greatly enjoy being the cigarette, which seemed to me no better than many I had smoked before.

"What do you think of my cigarettes?" he said, as I threw away the stump.

I felt that a blunt expression of opinion would be in bad taste after his generosity in offering an utter stranger the best he had. "Exquisite!" I answered.

"I thought you would say so," he replied, gravely. "Have another!"

"Let me try one of your common ones," I said.

"No, you shan't!" he replied, closing the case with a sudden snap, which endangered my fingers, but softening the *brusquerie* of the proceeding by one of his enthralling smiles; then he added, using one of the odd idioms which gave his speech a peculiar piquancy, "I don't palm off upon my friends what I have of second best." He re-opened the case and held it out to me. To have refused would have been to confess that I did not appreciate his "gems" as he called them. I smoked another, in which I still failed to find any unusual fragrance; but the aroma of my new-found friend's whole personality was so keen and subtle, that it may have deadened my nerves to any more material sensation.

We lay talking until the pink flush of evening spread along the horizon, and in it Corsica, invisible before, seemed to body itself forth from nothingness like an island of phantom peaks and headlands. Then we rose, and, in the quickly gathering dusk, took our way down among the olive-yards, and through the orange-gardens to Monte Carlo.

II

My acquaintance with my Fascinating Friend lasted little more than forty-eight hours, but during that time we were inseparable. He was not at my hotel, but on that first evening I persuaded him to dine with me, and soon after breakfast on the following morning I went in search of him; I was at the Russie, he at the Hôtel de Paris. I found him smoking in the veranda, and at a table not far distant sat the German of the previous afternoon, finishing a tolerably copious *déjeûner à la fourchette*. As soon as he had scraped his plate quite clean and finished the last dregs of his bottle of wine, he rose and took his way to the Casino. After a few minutes' talk with my Fascinating Friend, I suggested a stroll over to Monaco. He agreed, and we spent the whole day together, loitering and lounging, talking and dreaming. We went to the Casino in the afternoon to hear the concert, and I discovered my friend to be a cultivated musician. Then we strolled into the gambling-room for an hour, but neither of us played. The German was busy at one of the roulette-tables, and seemed to be winning considerably. That evening I dined with my friend at the table d'hôte of his hotel. At the other end of the table I could see the German sitting silent and unnoticing, rapt in the joys of deglutition.

Next morning, by arrangement, my friend called upon me at my hotel, and over one of his cigarettes, to which I was getting accustomed, we discussed our plan for the day. I suggested a wider flight than yesterday's. Had he ever been to Eza, the old Saracen robber-nest perched on a rock a thousand feet above the sea, halfway between Monaco and Villafranca? No, he had not been there, and after some consideration he agreed to accompany me. We went by rail to the little station on the seashore, and then attacked the arduous ascent. The day was perfect, though rather too warm for climbing, and we had frequent rests among the olive-trees, with delightfully discursive talks on all things under the sun. My companion's charm grew upon me moment by moment. There was in his manner a sort of refined coquetry of amiability which I found irresistible. It was combined with a frankness of sympathy and interest subtly flattering to a man of my unsocial habit of mind. I was conscious every now and then that he was drawing me out; but to be drawn out so gently and genially was, to me, a novel and delightful experience. It produced in me one of those effusions of communicativeness to which, I am told, all reticent people are occasionally subject. I have myself given way to them some three or four times in my life, and found myself pouring forth to perfect strangers such intimate details of feeling and experience as I would rather die than impart to my dearest friend. Three or four times, I say, have I found myself suddenly and inexplicably brought within the influence of some invisible truth-compelling talisman, which drew from me confessions the rack could not have extorted; but never has the influence been so irresistible as in the case of my Fascinating Friend. I told him what I had told to no other human soul — what I had told to the lonely glacier, to the lurid storm-cloud, to the seething sea, but had never breathed in mortal ear — I told him the tragedy of my life. How well I remember the scene! We were resting beneath the chestnut-trees that shadow a stretch of level sward immediately below the last short stage of ascent that leads into the heart of the squalid village now nestling in the crevices of the old Moslem fastness. The midday hush was on sea and sky. Far out on the horizon a level line of smoke showed where an unseen steamer was crawling along under the edge of the sapphire sphere. As I reached the climax of my tale an old woman, bent almost double beneath a huge fagot of firewood, passed us on her way to the village. I remember that it crossed my mind to wonder whether there was any capacity in the nature of such as she for suffering at all comparable to that which I was describing. My companion's sympathy was subtle and soothing. There was in my tale an element of the grotesque which might have tempted a vulgar nature to flippancy. No smile crossed my companion's lips. He turned away his head, on pretense of watching the receding figure of the old peasant-woman. When he looked at me again, his deep dark eyes were suffused with a moisture which enhanced the mystery of their tenderness. In that moment I felt, as I had never felt before, what it is to find a friend.

We returned to Monte Carlo late in the afternoon, and I found a telegram at my hotel begging me to be in Genoa the following morning. I had barely time to bundle my traps together and swallow a hasty meal before my train was due. I scrawled a note to my new found confidant, expressing most sincerely my sorrow at parting from him so soon and so suddenly, and my hope that ere long we should meet again.

III

The train was already at the platform when I reached the station. There were one or two first-class through carriages on it, which, for a French railway, were unusually empty. In one of them I saw at the window the head of the German, and from a certain subdued radiance in his expression, I judged that he must be carrying off a considerable "pile" from the gaming-table. His personality was not of the most attractive, and there was something in his squat nose suggestive of stertorous possibilities which, under ordinary circumstances, would have held me aloof from him. But — shall I confess it? — he had for me a certain sentimental attraction, because he was associated in my mind with that first meeting with my forty-eight hours' friend. I looked into his compartment; an overcoat and valise lay in the opposite corner from his, showing that seat to be engaged, but two corners were still left me to choose from. I installed myself in one of them, face to face with the valise and overcoat, and awaited the signal to start. The cry of "En voiture, messieurs!" soon came, and a lithe figure sprang into the carriage. It was my Fascinating Friend! For a single moment I thought that a flash of annoyance crossed his features on finding me there, but the impression vanished at once, for his greeting was as full of cordiality as of surprise. We soon exchanged explanations. He, like myself, had been called away by telegram, not to Genoa, but to Rome; he, like myself, had left a note expressing his heartfelt regret at our sudden separation. As we sped along, skirting bays that shone burnished in the evening light, and rumbling every now and then through a tunnel-pierced promontory, we resumed the almost affectionate converse interrupted only an hour before, and I found him a more delightful companion than ever. His exquisitely playful fantasy seemed to be acting at high pressure, as in the case of a man who is talking to pass the time under the stimulus of a delightful anticipation. I suspected that he was hurrying to some peculiarly agreeable rendezvous in Rome, and I hinted my suspicion, which he laughed off in such a way as to confirm it. The German, in the mean time, sat stolid and unmoved, making some pencilled calculations in a little pocket-book. He clearly did not understand English.

As we approached Ventimiglia my friend rose, took down his valise from the rack, and, turning his back to me, made some changes in its arrangement, which I, of course, did not see. He then locked it carefully and kept it beside him. At Ventimiglia we had all to turn out to undergo the inspection of the Italian *dogana*. My friend's valise was his sole luggage, and I noticed, rather to my surprise, that he gave the custom-house official a very large bribe — two or three gold pieces — to make his inspection of it purely nominal, and forego the opening of either of the inside compartments. The German, on the other hand, had a small portmanteau and a large dispatch box, both of which he opened with a certain ostentation, and I observed that the official's eyes glittered under his raised eyebrows as he looked into the contents of the dispatch-box. On returning to the train we all three resumed our old places, and the German drew the shade of a sleeping-cap over his eyes and settled himself down for the night. It was now quite dark, but the moon was shining.

"Have you a large supply of the 'gems' in your valise?" I asked, smiling, curious to know his reason for a subterfuge which accorded ill with his ordinary straight-forwardness, and remembering that tobacco is absolutely prohibited at the Italian frontier.

"Unfortunately, no," he said; "my 'gems' are all gone, and I have only my common cigarettes remaining. Will you try them, such as they are?" and he held out his case, both sides of which were now filled with the flat cigarettes. We each took one and lighted it, but he began giving me an account of a meeting he had had with Lord Beaconsfield, which he detailed so fully and with so much enthusiasm, that, after a whiff or two he allowed his cigarette to go out. I could not understand his taste in tobacco. These cigarettes which he despised seemed to me at once more delicate and more peculiar than the others. They had a flavour which was quite unknown to me. I was much interested in his vivid account of the personality of that great man, whom I admired then, while he was yet with us, and whom, as a knight of the Primrose League, I now revere; but our climb of the morning, and the scrambling departure of the afternoon, were beginning to tell on me, and I became irresistibly drowsy. Gradually, and in spite of myself, my eyes closed. I could still hear my companion's voice mingling with the heavy breathing of the German, who had been asleep for some time; but soon even these sounds ceased to penetrate the mist of languor, the end of my cigarette dropped from between my fingers and I knew no more.

*****

My awakening was slow and spasmodic. There was a clearly perceptible interval — probably several minutes — between the first stirrings of consciousness and the full clarification of my faculties. I began to be aware of the rumble and oscillation of the train without realizing what was meant. Then I opened my eyes and blinked at the lamp, and vaguely noted the yellow oil washing to and fro in the bowl. Then the white square of the "Avis aux Voyageurs" caught my eye in the gloom under the luggage-rack, and beneath it, on the seat, I saw the light reflected from the lock of the German's portmanteau. Next I was conscious of the German himself still sleeping in his corner, but no longer puffing and grunting as when I had fallen asleep. Then I raised my head, looked round the carriage, and the next moment sprang bolt upright in dismay.

Where was my Fascinating Friend?

Gone! vanished! There was not a trace of him. His valise, his great-coat, all had disappeared. Only in the little cigar-ash box on the window-frame I saw the flat cigarette which he had barely lighted — how long before? I looked at my watch: it must have been about an hour and a half ago.

By this time I had all my faculties about me. I looked across at the German, intending to ask him if he knew anything of our late travelling-companion. Then I noticed that his head had fallen forward in such a way that it seemed to me suffocation must be imminent. I approached him, and put down my head to look into his face. As I did so I saw a roundish black object on the oil-cloth floor not far from the toe of his boot. The lamplight was reflected at a single point from its convex surface. I put down my hand and touched it. It was liquid. I looked at my fingers — they were not black, but red. I think (but am not sure) that I screamed aloud. I shrank to the other end of the carriage, and it was some moments before I had sufficient presence of mind to look for a means of communicating with the guard. Of course there was none. I was alone for an indefinite time with a dead man. But was he dead? I had little doubt, from the way his head hung, that his throat was cut, and a horrible fascination drew me to his side to examine. No; there was no sign of the hideous fissure I expected to find beneath the gray bristles of his beard. His head fell forward again into the same position, and I saw with horror that I had left two bloody fingermarks upon the gray shade of his sleeping-cap. Then I noticed for the first time that the window he was facing stood open, for a gust of wind came through it and blew back the lapel of his coat. What was that on his waistcoat? I tore the coat back and examined: it was a small triangular hole just over the heart, and round it there was a dark circle about the size of a shilling, where the blood had soaked through the light material. In examining it I did what the murderer had not done — disturbed the equilibrium of the body, which fell over against me.

At that moment I heard a loud voice behind me, coming from I knew not where. I nearly fainted with terror. The train was still going at full speed; the compartment was empty, save for myself and the ghastly object which lay in my arms; and yet I seemed to hear a voice almost at my ear. There it was again! I summoned up courage to look round. It was the guard of the train clinging on outside the window and demanding "Biglietti!" By this time, he, too, saw that something was amiss. He opened the door and swung himself into the carriage. "Dio mio!" I heard him exclaim, as I actually flung myself into his arms and pointed to the body now lying in a huddled heap amid its own blood on the floor. Then, for the first time in my life, I positively swooned away, and knew no more.

When I came to myself the train had stopped at a small station, the name of which I do not know to this day. There was a Babel of speech going on around, not one word of which I could understand. I was on the platform, supported between two men in uniform, with cocked hats and cockades. In vain I tried to tell my story. I knew little or no Italian, and, though there were one or two Frenchmen in the train, they were useless as interpreters, for on the one hand my power of speaking French seemed to have departed in my agitation, and on the other hand none of the Italians understood it. In vain I tried to make them understand that a "giovane" had travelled in the compartment with us who had now disappeared. The Italian guard, who had come on at Ventimiglia, evidently had no recollection of him. He merely shook his head, said "Non capisco," and inquired if I was "Prussiano." The train had already been delayed some time, and, after a consultation between the station-master, the guard, the syndic of the village, who had been summoned in haste, it was determined to hand the matter over to the authorities at Genoa. The two carabinieri sat one on each side of me facing the engine, and on the opposite seat the body was stretched out with a luggage tarpaulin over it. In this hideous fashion I passed the four or five remaining hours of the journey to Genoa.

The next week I spent in an Italian prison, a very uncomfortable yet quite unromantic place of abode. Fortunately, my friends were by this time in Genoa, and they succeeded in obtaining some slight mitigation of my discomforts. At the end of that time I was released, there being no evidence against me. The testimony of the French guard, of the booking-clerk at Monaco, and of the staff of the Hôtel de Paris, established the existence of my Fascinating Friend, which was at first called in question; but no trace could be found of him. With him had disappeared his victim's dispatch-box, in which were stored the proceeds of several days of successful gambling. Robbery, however, did not seem to have been the primary motive of the crime, for his watch, purse, and the heavy jewelry about his person were all untouched. From the German Consul at Genoa I learned privately, after my release, that the murdered man, though in fact a Prussian, had lived long in Russia, and was suspected of having had an unofficial connection with the St. Petersburg police. It was thought, indeed, that the capital with which he had commenced his operation at Monte Carlo was the reward of some special act of treachery; so that the anarchists, if it was indeed they who struck the blow, had merely suffered Judas to put his thirty pieces out to usance, in order to pay back to their enemies with interest the blood-money of their friends.

IV

About two years later I happened one day to make an afternoon call in Mayfair, at the house of a lady well known in the social and political world, who honours me, if I may say so, with her friendship. Her drawing-room was crowded, and the cheerful ring of afternoon tea-cups was audible through the pleasant medley of women's voices. I joined a group around the hostess, where an animated discussion was in progress on the Irish Coercion Bill, then the leading political topic of the day. The argument interested me deeply; but it is one of my mental peculiarities that when several conversations are going on around me I can by no means keep my attention exclusively fixed upon the one in which I am myself engaged. Odds and ends from all the others find their way into my ears and my consciousness, and I am sometimes accused of absence of mind, when my fault is in reality a too great alertness of the sense of hearing. In this instance the conversation of three or four groups was more or less audible to me; but it was not long before my attention was absorbed by the voice of a lady, seated at the other side of the circular ottoman on which I myself had taken my place.

She was talking merrily, and her hearers, in one of whom, as I glanced over my shoulder, I recognized an ex-Cabinet Minister, seemed to be greatly entertained. As her back was toward me, all I could see of the lady herself was her short black hair falling over the handsome fur collar of her mantle.

"He was so tragic about it," she was saying, "that it was really *impayable*. The lady was beautiful, wealthy, accomplished, and I don't know what else. The rival was an Australian squatter, with a beard as thick as his native bush. My communicative friend — I scarcely knew even his name when he poured forth his woes to me — thought that he had an advantage in his light moustache, with a military twirl in it. They were all three travelling in Switzerland, but the Australian had gone off to make the ascent of some peak or other, leaving the field to the foe for a couple of days at least. On the first day the foe made the most of his time, and had nearly brought matters to a crisis. The next morning he got himself up as exquisitely as possible, in order to clinch his conquest, but found to his disgust that he had left his dressing-case with his razors at the last stopping-place. There was nothing for it but to try the village barber, who was also the village stationer, and draper, and ironmonger, and chemist — a sort of Alpine Whiteley, in fact. His face had just been soaped — what do you call it? — lathered, is it not? and the barber had actually taken hold of his nose so as to get his head into the right position, when, in the mirror opposite, he saw the door open, and — oh, horror! — who should walk into the shop but the fair one herself! He gave such a start that the barber gashed his chin. His eyes met hers in the mirror; for a moment he saw her lips quiver and tremble, and then she burst into shrieks of uncontrollable laughter, and rushed out of the shop. If you knew the pompous little man, I am sure you would sympathize with her. I know I did when he told me the story. His heart sank within him, but he acted like a Briton. He determined to take no notice of the *contretemps*, but return boldly to the attack. She received him demurely at first, but the moment she raised her eyes to his face, and saw the patch of sticking-plaster on his chin, she was again seized with such convulsions that she had to rush from the room. 'She is now in Melbourne,' he said, almost with a sob, 'and I assure you, my dear friend, that I never now touch a razor without an impulse, to which I expect I shall one day succumb, to put it to a desperate use.'"

There was a singing in my ears, and my brain was whirling. This story, heartlessly and irreverently told, was the tragedy of my life!

I had breathed it to no human soul — *save one*!

I rose from my seat, wondering within myself whether my agitation was visible to those around me, and went over to the other side of the room whence I could obtain a view of the speaker. There were the deep, dark eyes, there were the full sensuous lips, the upper shaded with an impalpable down, there was the charcoal-black hair! I knew too well that rich contralto voice! It was my Fascinating Friend!

Before I had fully realized the situation she rose, handed her empty tea-cup to the Cabinet-Minister, bowed to him and his companion, and made her way up to the hostess, evidently intending to take her leave. As she turned away, after shaking hands cordially with Lady X— — , her eyes met mine intently fixed upon her. She did not start, she neither flushed nor turned pale; she simply raised for an instant her finely arched eyebrows, and as her tall figure sailed past me out of the room, she turned upon me the same exquisite and irresistible smile with which my Fascinating Friend had offered me his cigarette-case that evening among the olive-trees.

I hurried up to Lady X— — .

"Who is the lady who has just left the room?" I asked.

"Oh, that is the Baroness M— — ," she replied. "She is half an Englishwoman, half a Pole. She was my daughter's bosom friend at Girton — a most interesting girl."

"Is she a politician?" I asked.

"No; that's the one thing I don't like about her. She is not a bit of a patriot; she makes a joke of her country's wrongs and sufferings. Should you like to meet her? Dine with us the day after to-morrow. She is to be here."

*****

I dined at Lady X— — 's on the appointed day, but the Baroness was not there. Urgent family affairs had called her suddenly to Poland.

A week later the assassination of the Czar sent a thrill of horror through the civilized world.

*****

"Don't you think your friend might be held an

accessory after the fact to the death of the German?" asked the Novelist, when all the flattering comments, which were many, were at an end. "And an accessory before the fact to the assassination of the Czar?" chimed in the Editor. "Why didn't he go straight from Lady— — 's house to the nearest police-station and put the police on the track of his 'Fascinating Friend'?" "What a question!" the Romancer exclaimed, starting from his seat and pacing restlessly about the deck. "How could any man with a palate for the rarest flavours of life resist the temptation of taking that woman down to dinner? And, besides, hadn't he eaten salt with her? Hadn't he smoked the social cigarette with her? Shade of De Quincey! are we to treat like a vulgar criminal a mistress of the finest of the fine arts? Shall we be such crawling creatures as to seek to lay by the heels a Muse of Murder? Are we a generation of detectives, that we should do this thing?" "So my friend put it to me," said the Critic dryly, "not quite so eloquently, but to that effect. Between ourselves, though, I believe he was influenced more by consideration of his personal safety than by admiration for murder as a fine art. He remembered the fate of the German, and was unwilling to share it." "He adopted a policy of non-intervention," said the Eminent Tragedian, who in his hours of leisure, was something of a politician. "I should rather say of *laissez faire*, or, more precisely, of *laissez assassiner*," laughed the Editor. "What was the Fascinating Friend supposed to have in her portmanteau?" asked Beatrice. "What was she so anxious to conceal from the custom-house officers?" "Her woman's clothes, I imagine," the Critic replied, "though I don't hold myself bound to explain all the ins and outs of her proceedings." "Then she *was* a wonderful woman," replied the fair questioner, as one having authority, "if she could get a respectable gown and 'fixings,' as the Americans say, into a small portmanteau. But," she added, "I very soon suspected she was a woman." "Why?" asked several voices simultaneously. "Why, because she drew him out so easily," was the reply. "You think, in fact," said the Romancer, "that however little its victim was aware of it, there was a touch of the *Ewig-weibliche* in her fascination?" "Precisely."

IX. The Lost Room — Fitz-James O'Brien

It was oppressively warm. The sun had long disappeared, but seemed to have left its vital spirit of heat behind it. The air rested; the leaves of the acacia-trees that shrouded my windows hung plumb-like on their delicate stalks. The smoke of my cigar scarce rose above my head, but hung about me in a pale blue cloud, which I had to dissipate with languid waves of my hand. My shirt was open at the throat, and my chest heaved laboriously in the effort to catch some breaths of fresher air. The noises of the city seemed to be wrapped in slumber, and the shrilling of the mosquitos was the only sound that broke the stillness.

As I lay with my feet elevated on the back of a chair, wrapped in that peculiar frame of mind in which thought assumes a species of lifeless motion, the strange fancy seized me of making a languid inventory of the principal articles of furniture in my room. It was a task well suited to the mood in which I found myself. Their forms were duskily defined in the dim twilight that floated shadowily through the chamber; it was no labour to note and particularize each, and from the place where I sat I could command a view of all my possessions without even turning my head.

There was, *imprimis*, that ghostly lithograph by Calame. It was a mere black spot on the white wall, but my inner vision scrutinized every detail of the picture. A wild, desolate, midnight heath, with a spectral oak-tree in the centre of the foreground. The wind blows fiercely, and the jagged branches, clothed scantily with ill-grown leaves, are swept to the left continually by its giant force.

A formless wrack of clouds streams across the awful sky, and the rain sweeps almost parallel with the horizon. Beyond, the heath stretches off into endless blackness, in the extreme of which either fancy or art has conjured up some undefinable shapes that seem riding into space. At the base of the huge oak stands a shrouded figure. His mantle is wound by the blast in tight folds around his form, and the long cock's feather in his hat is blown upright, till it seems as if it stood on end with fear. His features are not visible, for he has grasped his cloak with both hands, and drawn it from either side across his face. The picture is seemingly objectless. It tells no tale, but there is a weird power about it that haunts one, and it was for that I bought it.

Next to the picture comes the round blot that hangs below it, which I know to be a smoking-cap. It has my coat of arms embroidered on the front, and for that reason I never wear it; though, when properly arranged on my head, with its long blue silken tassel hanging down by my cheek, I believe it becomes me well. I remember the time when it was in the course of manufacture. I remember the tiny little hands that pushed the coloured silks so nimbly through the cloth that was stretched on the embroidery-frame, — the vast trouble I was put to to get a coloured copy of my armorial bearings for the heraldic work which was to decorate the front of the band, — the pursings up of the little mouth, and the contractions of the young forehead, as their possessor plunged into a profound sea of cogitation touching the way in which the cloud should be represented from which the armed hand, that is my crest, issues, — the heavenly moment when the tiny hands placed it on my head, in a position that I could not bear for more than a few seconds, and I, kinglike, immediately assumed my royal prerogative after the coronation, and instantly levied a tax on my only subjects which was, however, not paid unwillingly. Ah! the cap is there, but the embroiderer has fled; for Atropos was severing the web of life above her head while she was weaving that silken shelter for mine!

How uncouthly the huge piano that occupies the corner at the left of the door looms out in the uncertain twilight! I neither play nor sing, yet I own a piano. It is a comfort to me to look at it, and to feel that the music is there, although I am not able to break the spell that binds it. It is pleasant to know that Bellini and Mozart, Cimarosa, Porpora, Glück and all such, — or at least their souls, — sleep in that unwieldy case. There lie embalmed, as it were, all operas, sonatas, oratorios, nocturnos, marches, songs and dances, that ever climbed into existence through the four bars that wall in melody. Once I was entirely repaid for the investment of my funds in that instrument which I never use. Blokeeta, the composer, came to see me. Of course his instincts urged him as irresistibly to my piano as if some magnetic power lay within it compelling him to approach. He tuned it, he played on it. All night long, until the gray and spectral dawn rose out of the depths of the midnight, he sat and played, and I lay smoking by the window listening. Wild, unearthly, and sometimes insufferably painful, were the improvisations of Blokeeta. The chords of the instrument seemed breaking with anguish. Lost souls shrieked in his dismal preludes; the half-heard utterances of spirits in pain, that groped at inconceivable distances from anything lovely or harmonious, seemed to rise dimly up out of the waves of sound that gathered under his hands. Melancholy human love wandered out on distant heaths, or beneath dank and gloomy cypresses, murmuring its unanswered sorrow, or hateful gnomes sported and sang in the stagnant swamps triumphing in unearthly tones over the knight whom they had lured to his death. Such was Blokeeta's night's entertainment; and when he at length closed the piano, and hurried away through the cold morning, he left a memory about the instrument from which I could never escape.

Those snow-shoes that hang in the space between the mirror and the door recall Canadian wanderings, — a long race through the dense forests, over the frozen snow through whose brittle crust the slender hoofs of the caribou that we were pursuing sank at every step, until the poor creature despairingly turned at bay in a small juniper coppice, and we heartlessly shot him down. And I remember how Gabriel, the *habitant*, and François, the half-breed, cut his throat, and how the hot blood rushed out in a torrent over the snowy soil; and I recall the snow *cabane* that Gabriel built, where we all three slept so warmly; and the great fire that glowed at our feet, painting all kinds of demoniac shapes on the black screen of forest that lay without; and the deer-steaks that we roasted for our breakfast; and the savage drunkenness of Gabriel in the morning, he having been privately drinking out of my brandy-flask all the night long.

That long haftless dagger that dangles over the mantelpiece makes my heart swell. I found it, when a boy, in a hoary old castle in which one of my maternal ancestors once lived. That same ancestor — who, by the way, yet lives in history — was a strange old sea-king, who dwelt on the extremest point of the southwestern coast of Ireland. He owned the whole of that fertile island called Inniskeiran, which directly faces Cape Clear, where between them the Atlantic rolls furiously, forming what the fishermen of the place call "the Sound." An awful place in winter is that same Sound. On certain days no boat can live there for a moment, and Cape Clear is frequently cut off for days from any communication with the mainland.

This old sea-king — Sir Florence O'Driscoll by name — passed a stormy life. From the summit of his castle he watched the ocean, and when any richly laden vessels bound from the South to the industrious Galway merchants, hove in sight, Sir Florence hoisted the sails of his galley, and it went hard with him if he did not tow into harbor ship and crew. In this way he lived; not a very honest mode of livelihood, certainly, according to our modern ideas, but quite reconcilable with the morals of the time. As may be supposed, Sir Florence got into trouble. Complaints were laid against him at the English court by the plundered merchants, and the Irish viking set out for London, to plead his own cause before good Queen Bess, as she was called. He had one powerful recommendation: he was a marvellously handsome man. Not Celtic by descent, but half Spanish, half Danish in blood, he had the great northern stature with the regular features, flashing eyes, and dark hair of the Iberian race. This may account for the fact that his stay at the English court was much longer than was necessary, as also for the tradition, which a local historian mentions, that the English Queen evinced a preference for the Irish chieftain, of other nature than that usually shown by monarch to subject.

Previous to his departure, Sir Florence had intrusted the care of his property to an Englishman named Hull. During the long absence of the knight, this person managed to ingratiate himself with the local authorities, and gain their favour so far that they were willing to support him in almost any scheme. After a protracted stay, Sir Florence, pardoned of all his misdeeds, returned to his home. Home no longer. Hull was in possession, and refused to yield an acre of the lands he had so nefariously acquired. It was no use appealing to the law, for its officers were in the opposite interest. It was no use appealing to the Queen, for she had another lover, and had forgotten the poor Irish knight by this time; and so the viking passed the best portion of his life in unsuccessful attempts to reclaim his vast estates, and was eventually, in his old age, obliged to content himself with his castle by the sea and the island of Inniskeiran, the only spot of which the usurper was unable to deprive him. So this old story of my kinsman's fate looms up out of the darkness that enshrouds that haftless dagger hanging on the wall.

It was somewhat after the foregoing fashion that I dreamily made the inventory of my personal property. As I turned my eyes on each object, one after the other, — or the places where they lay, for the room was now so dark that it was almost impossible to see with any distinctness, — a crowd of memories connected with each rose up before me, and, perforce, I had to indulge them. So I proceeded but slowly, and at last my cigar shortened to a hot and bitter morsel that I could barely hold between my lips, while it seemed to me that the night grew each moment more insufferably oppressive. While I was revolving some impossible means of cooling my wretched body, the cigar stump began to burn my lips. I flung it angrily through the open window, and stooped out to watch it falling. It first lighted on the leaves of the acacia, sending out a spray of red sparkles, then, rolling off, it fell plump on the dark walk in the garden, faintly illuminating for a moment the dusky trees and breathless flowers. Whether it was the contrast between the red flash of the cigar-stump and the silent darkness of the garden, or whether it was that I detected by the sudden light a faint waving of the leaves, I know not; but something suggested to me that the garden was cool. I will take a turn there, thought I, just as I am; it cannot be warmer than this room, and however still the atmosphere, there is always a feeling of liberty and spaciousness in the open air, that partially supplies one's wants. With this idea running through my head, I arose, lit another cigar, and passed out into the long, intricate corridors that led to the main staircase. As I crossed the threshold of my room, with what a different feeling I should have passed it had I known that I was never to set foot in it again!

I lived in a very large house, in which I occupied two rooms on the second floor. The house was old-fashioned, and all the floors communicated by a huge circular staircase that wound up through the centre of the building, while at every landing long, rambling corridors stretched off into mysterious nooks and corners. This palace of mine was very high, and its resources, in the way of crannies and windings, seemed to be interminable. Nothing seemed to stop anywhere. Cul-de-sacs were unknown on the premises. The corridors and passages, like mathematical lines, seemed capable of indefinite extension, and the object of the architect must have been to erect an edifice in which people might go ahead forever. The whole place was gloomy, not so much because it was large, but because an unearthly nakedness seemed to pervade the structure. The staircases, corridors, halls, and vestibules all partook of a desert-like desolation. There was nothing on the walls to break the sombre monotony of those long vistas of shade. No carvings on the wainscoting, no moulded masks peering down from the simply severe cornices, no marble vases on the landings. There was an eminent dreariness and want of life — so rare in an American establishment — all over the abode. It was Hood's haunted house put in order and newly painted. The servants, too, were shadowy, and chary of their visits. Bells rang three times before the gloomy chambermaid could be induced to present herself; and the negro waiter, a ghoul-like looking creature from Congo, obeyed the summons only when one's patience was exhausted or one's want satisfied in some other way. When he did come, one felt sorry that he had not stayed away altogether, so sullen and savage did he appear. He moved along the echoless floors with a slow, noiseless shamble, until his dusky figure, advancing from the gloom, seemed like some reluctant afreet, compelled by the superior power of his master to disclose himself. When the doors of all the chambers were closed, and no light illuminated the long corridor save the red, unwholesome glare of a small oil lamp on a table at the end, where late lodgers lit their candles, one could not by any possibility conjure up a sadder or more desolate prospect.

Yet the house suited me. Of meditative and sedentary habits, I enjoyed the extreme quiet. There were but few lodgers, from which I infer that the landlord did not drive a very thriving trade; and these, probably oppressed by the sombre spirit of the place, were quiet and ghost-like in their movements. The proprietor I scarcely ever saw. My bills were deposited by unseen hands every month on my table, while I was out walking or riding, and my pecuniary response was intrusted to the attendant afreet. On the whole, when the bustling, wide-awake spirit of New York is taken into consideration, the sombre, half-vivified character of the house in which I lived was an anomaly that no one appreciated better than I who lived there.

I felt my way down the wide, dark staircase in my pursuit of zephyrs. The garden, as I entered it, did feel somewhat cooler than my own room, and I puffed my cigar along the dim, cypress-shrouded walks with a sensation of comparative relief. It was very dark. The tall-growing flowers that bordered the path were so wrapped in gloom as to present the aspect of solid pyramidal masses, all the details of leaves and blossoms being buried in an embracing darkness, while the trees had lost all form, and seemed like masses of overhanging cloud. It was a place and time to excite the imagination; for in the impenetrable cavities of endless gloom there was room for the most riotous fancies to play at will. I walked and walked, and the echoes of my footsteps on the ungravelled and mossy path suggested a double feeling. I felt alone and yet in company at the same time. The solitariness of the place made itself distinct enough in the stillness, broken alone by the hollow reverberations of my step, while those very reverberations seemed to imbue me with an undefined feeling that I was not alone. I was not, therefore, much startled when I was suddenly accosted from beneath the solid darkness of an immense cypress by a voice saying, "Will you give me a light, sir?"

"Certainly," I replied, trying in vain to distinguish the speaker amidst the impenetrable dark.

Somebody advanced, and I held out my cigar. All I could gather definitively about the individual who thus accosted me was that he must have been of extremely small stature; for I, who am by no means an overgrown man, had to stoop considerably in handing him my cigar. The vigorous puff that he gave his own lighted up my Havana for a moment, and I fancied that I caught a glimpse of long, wild hair. The flash was, however, so momentary that I could not even say certainly whether this was an actual impression or the mere effort of imagination to embody that which the senses had failed to distinguish.

"Sir, you are out late," said this unknown to me, as he, with half-uttered thanks, handed me back my cigar, for which I had to grope in the gloom.

"Not later than usual," I replied, dryly.

"Hum! you are fond of late wanderings, then?"

"That is just as the fancy seizes me."

"Do you live here?"

"Yes."

"Queer house, isn't it?"

"I have only found it quiet."

"Hum! But you *will* find it queer, take my word for it." This was earnestly uttered; and I felt at the same time a bony finger laid on my arm, that cut it sharply like a blunted knife.

"I cannot take your word for any such assertion," I replied rudely, shaking off the bony finger with an irrepressible motion of disgust.

"No offence, no offence," muttered my unseen companion rapidly, in a strange, subdued voice, that would have been shrill had it been louder; "your being angry does not alter the matter. You will find it a queer house. Everybody finds it a queer house. Do you know who live there?"

"I never busy myself, sir, about other people's affairs," I answered sharply, for the individual's manner, combined with my utter uncertainty as to his appearance, oppressed me with an irksome longing to be rid of him.

"O, you don't? Well, I do. I know what they are — well, well, well!" and as he pronounced the three last words his voice rose with each, until, with the last, it reached a shrill shriek that echoed horribly among the lonely walks. "Do you know what they eat?" he continued.

"No, sir, — nor care."

"O, but you will care. You must care. You shall care. I'll tell you what they are. They are enchanters. They are ghouls. They are cannibals. Did you never remark their eyes, and how they gloated on you when you passed? Did you never remark the food that they served up at your table? Did you never in the dead of night hear muffled and unearthly footsteps gliding along the corridors, and stealthy hands turning the handle of your door? Does not some magnetic influence fold itself continually around you when they pass, and send a thrill through spirit and body, and a cold shiver that no sunshine will chase away? O, you have! You have felt all these things! I know it!"

The earnest rapidity, the subdued tones, the eagerness of accent, with which all this was uttered, impressed me most uncomfortably. It really seemed as if I could recall all those weird occurrences and influences of which he spoke; and I shuddered in spite of myself in the midst of the impenetrable darkness that surrounded me.

"Hum!" said I, assuming, without knowing it, a confidential tone, "may I ask you how you know these things?"

"How I know them? Because I am their enemy; because they tremble at my whisper; because I hang upon their track with the perseverance of a bloodhound and the stealthiness of a tiger; because — because — I was *of* them once!"

"Wretch!" I cried excitedly, for involuntarily his eager tones had wrought me up to a high pitch of spasmodic nervousness, "then you mean to say that you — — "

As I uttered this word, obeying an uncontrollable impulse, I stretched forth my hand in the direction of the speaker and made a blind clutch. The tips of my fingers seemed to touch a surface as smooth as glass, that glided suddenly from under them. A sharp, angry hiss sounded through the gloom, followed by a whirring noise, as if some projectile passed rapidly by, and the next moment I felt instinctively that I was alone.

A most disagreeable feeling instantly assailed me; — a prophetic instinct that some terrible misfortune menaced me; an eager and overpowering anxiety to get back to my own room without loss of time. I turned and ran blindly along the dark cypress alley, every dusky clump of flowers that rose blackly in the borders making my heart each moment cease to beat. The echoes of my own footsteps seemed to redouble and assume the sounds of unknown pursuers following fast upon my track. The boughs of lilac-bushes and syringas, that here and there stretched partly across the walk, seemed to have been furnished suddenly with hooked hands that sought to grasp me as I flew by, and each moment I expected to behold some awful and impassable barrier fall across my track and wall me up forever.

At length I reached the wide entrance. With a single leap I sprang up the four or five steps that formed the stoop, and dashed along the hall, up the wide, echoing stairs, and again along the dim, funereal corridors until I paused, breathless and panting, at the door of my room. Once so far, I stopped for an instant and leaned heavily against one of the panels, panting lustily after my late run. I had, however, scarcely rested my whole weight against the door, when it suddenly gave way, and I staggered in head-foremost. To my utter astonishment the room I had left in profound darkness was now a blaze of light. So intense was the illumination that, for a few seconds while the pupils of my eyes were contracting under the sudden change, I saw absolutely nothing save the dazzling glare. This fact in itself, coming on me with such utter suddenness, was sufficient to prolong my confusion, and it was not until after several minutes had elapsed that I perceived the room was not only illuminated, but occupied. And such occupants! Amazement at the scene took such possession of me that I was incapable of either moving or uttering a word. All that I could do was to lean against the wall, and stare blankly at the strange picture.

It might have been a scene out of Faublas, or Gramont's Memoirs, or happened in some palace of

Minister Foucque.

Round a large table in the centre of the room, where I had left a student-like litter of books and papers, were seated half a dozen persons. Three were men and three were women. The table was heaped with a prodigality of luxuries. Luscious eastern fruits were piled up in silver filigree vases, through whose meshes their glowing rinds shone in the contrasts of a thousand hues. Small silver dishes that Benvenuto might have designed, filled with succulent and aromatic meats, were distributed upon a cloth of snowy damask. Bottles of every shape, slender ones from the Rhine, stout fellows from Holland, sturdy ones from Spain, and quaint basket-woven flasks from Italy, absolutely littered the board. Drinking-glasses of every size and hue filled up the interstices, and the thirsty German flagon stood side by side with the aërial bubbles of Venetian glass that rest so lightly on their threadlike stems. An odour of luxury and sensuality floated through the apartment. The lamps that burned in every direction seemed to diffuse a subtle incense on the air, and in a large vase that stood on the floor I saw a mass of magnolias, tuberoses, and jasmines grouped together, stifling each other with their honeyed and heavy fragrance.

The inhabitants of my room seemed beings well suited to so sensual an atmosphere. The women were strangely beautiful, and all were attired in dresses of the most fantastic devices and brilliant hues. Their figures were round, supple, and elastic; their eyes dark and languishing; their lips full, ripe, and of the richest bloom. The three men wore half-masks, so that all I could distinguish were heavy jaws, pointed beards, and brawny throats that rose like massive pillars out of their doublets. All six lay reclining on Roman couches about the table, drinking down the purple wines in large draughts, and tossing back their heads and laughing wildly.

I stood, I suppose, for some three minutes, with my back against the wall staring vacantly at the bacchanal vision, before any of the revellers appeared to notice my presence. At length, without any expression to indicate whether I had been observed from the beginning or not, two of the women arose from their couches, and, approaching, took each a hand and led me to the table. I obeyed their motions mechanically. I sat on a couch, between them as they indicated. I unresistingly permitted them to wind their arms about my neck.

"You must drink," said one, pouring out a large glass of red wine, "here is Clos Vougeout of a rare vintage; and here," pushing a flask of amber-hued wine before me, "is Lachryma Christi."

"You must eat," said the other, drawing the silver dishes toward her. "Here are cutlets stewed with olives, and here are slices of a *filet* stuffed with bruised sweet chestnuts" — and as she spoke, she, without waiting for a reply, proceeded to help me.

The sight of the food recalled to me the warnings I had received in the garden. This sudden effort of memory restored to me my other faculties at the same instant. I sprang to my feet, thrusting the women from me with each hand.

"Demons!" I almost shouted. "I will have none of your accursed food. I know you. You are cannibals, you are ghouls, you are enchanters. Begone, I tell you! Leave my room in peace!"

A shout of laughter from all six was the only effect that my passionate speech produced. The men rolled on their couches, and their half-masks quivered with the convulsions of their mirth. The women shrieked, and tossed the slender wine-glasses wildly aloft, and turned to me and flung themselves on my bosom fairly sobbing with laughter.

"Yes," I continued, as soon as the noisy mirth had subsided, "yes, I say, leave my room instantly! I will have none of your unnatural orgies here!"

"His room!" shrieked the woman on my right.

"His room!" echoed she on my left.

"His room! He calls it his room!" shouted the whole party, as they rolled once more into jocular convulsions.

"How know you that it is your room?" said one of the men who sat opposite to me, at length, after the laughter had once more somewhat subsided.

"How do I know?" I replied indignantly. "How do I know my own room? How could I mistake it, pray? There's my furniture — my piano — — "

"He calls that a piano," shouted my neighbours, again in convulsions as I pointed to the corner where my huge piano, sacred to the memory of Blokeeta, used to stand. "O, yes! It is his room. There — there is his piano!"

The peculiar emphasis they laid on the word "piano" caused me to scrutinize the article I was indicating more thoroughly. Up to this time, though utterly amazed at the entrance of these people into my chamber, and connecting them somewhat with the wild stories I had heard in the garden, I still had a sort of indefinite idea that the whole thing was a masquerading freak got up in my absence, and that the bacchanalian orgie I was witnessing was nothing more than a portion of some elaborate hoax of which I was to be the victim. But when my eyes turned to the corner where I had left a huge and cumbrous piano, and beheld a vast and sombre organ lifting its fluted front to the very ceiling, and convinced myself, by a hurried process of memory, that it occupied the very spot in which I had left my own instrument, the little self-possession that I had left forsook me. I gazed around me bewildered.

In like manner everything was changed. In the place of that old haftless dagger, connected with so many historic associations personal to myself, I beheld a Turkish yataghan dangling by its belt of crimson silk, while the jewels in the hilt blazed as the lamplight played upon them. In the spot where hung my cherished smoking cap, memorial of a buried love, a knightly casque was suspended on the crest of which a golden dragon stood in the act of springing. That strange lithograph of Calame was no longer a lithograph, but it seemed to me that the portion of the wall which it covered, of the exact shape and size, had been cut out, and, in place of the picture, a *real* scene on the same scale, and with real actors, was distinctly visible. The old oak was there, and the stormy sky was there; but I saw the branches of the oak sway with the tempest, and the clouds drive before the wind. The wanderer in his cloak was gone; but in his place I beheld a circle of wild figures, men and women, dancing with linked hands around the hole of the great tree, chanting some wild fragment of a song, to which the winds roared an unearthly chorus. The snow-shoes, too, on whose sinewy woof I had sped for many days amidst Canadian wastes, had vanished, and in their place lay a pair of strange up-curled Turkish slippers, that had, perhaps, been many a time shuffled off at the doors of mosques, beneath the steady blaze of an orient sun.

All was changed. Wherever my eyes turned they missed familiar objects, yet encountered strange representatives. Still, in all the substitutes there seemed to me a reminiscence of what they replaced. They seemed only for a time transmuted into other shapes, and there lingered around them the atmosphere of what they once had been. Thus I could have sworn the room to have been mine, yet there was nothing in it that I could rightly claim. Everything reminded me of some former possession that it was not. I looked for the acacia at the window, and lo! long silken palm-leaves swayed in through the open lattice; yet they had the same motion and the same air of my favourite tree, and seemed to murmur to me, "Though we seem to be palm-leaves, yet are we acacia-leaves; yea, those very ones on which you used to watch the butterflies alight and the rain patter while you smoked and dreamed!" So in all things; the room was, yet was not, mine; and a sickening consciousness of my utter inability to reconcile its identity with its appearance overwhelmed me, and choked my reason.

"Well, have you determined whether or not this is your room?" asked the girl on my left, proffering me a huge tumbler creaming over with champagne, and laughing wickedly as she spoke.

"It is mine," I answered, doggedly, striking the glass rudely with my hand, and dashing the aromatic wine over the white cloth. "I know that it is mine; and ye are jugglers and enchanters who want to drive me mad."

"Hush! hush!" she said, gently, not in the least angered by my rough treatment. "You are excited.

Alf shall play something to soothe you."

At her signal, one of the men sat down at the organ. After a short, wild, spasmodic prelude, he began what seemed to me to be a symphony of recollections. Dark and sombre, and all through full of quivering and intense agony, it appeared to recall a dark and dismal night, on a cold reef, around which an unseen but terribly audible ocean broke with eternal fury. It seemed as if a lonely pair were on the reef, one living, the other dead; one clasping his arms around the tender neck and naked bosom of the other, striving to warm her into life, when his own vitality was being each moment sucked from him by the icy breath of the storm. Here and there a terrible wailing minor key would tremble through the chords like the shriek of sea-birds, or the warning of advancing death. While the man played I could scarce restrain myself. It seemed to be Blokeeta whom I listened to, and on whom I gazed. That wondrous night of pleasure and pain that I had once passed listening to him seemed to have been taken up again at the spot where it had broken off, and the same hand was continuing it. I stared at the man called Alf. There he sat with his cloak and doublet, and long rapier and mask of black velvet. But there was something in the air of the peaked beard, a familiar mystery in the wild mass of raven hair that fell as if wind-blown over his shoulders, which riveted my memory.

"Blokeeta! Blokeeta!" I shouted, starting up furiously from the couch on which I was lying, and bursting the fair arms that were linked around my neck as if they had been hateful chains, — "Blokeeta! my friend! speak to me, I entreat you! Tell these horrid enchanters to leave me. Say that I hate them. Say that I command them to leave my room."

The man at the organ stirred not in answer to my appeal. He ceased playing, and the dying sound of the last note he had touched faded off into a melancholy moan. The other men and the women burst once more into peals of mocking laughter.

"Why will you persist in calling this your room?" said the woman next me, with a smile meant to be kind, but to me inexpressibly loathsome. "Have we not shown you by the furniture, by the general appearance of the place, that you are mistaken, and that this cannot be your apartment? Rest content, then, with us. You are welcome here, and need no longer trouble yourself about your room."

"Rest content!" I answered madly; "live with ghosts, eat of awful meats, and see awful sights! Never! never! You have cast some enchantment over the place that has disguised it; but for all that I know it to be my room. You shall leave it!"

"Softly, softly!" said another of the sirens. "Let us settle this amicably. This poor gentleman seems obstinate and inclined to make an uproar. Now we do not want an uproar. We love the night and its quiet; and there is no night that we love so well as that on which the moon is coffined in clouds. Is it not so, my brothers?"

An awful and sinister smile gleamed on the countenances of her unearthly audience, and seemed to glide visibly from underneath their masks.

"Now," she continued, "I have a proposition to make. It would be ridiculous for us to surrender this room simply because this gentleman states that it is his; and yet I feel anxious to gratify, as far as may be fair, his wild assertion of ownership. A room, after all, is not much to us; we can get one easily enough, but still we should be loath to give this apartment up to so imperious a demand. We are willing, however, to *risk* its loss. That is to say," — turning to me, — "I propose that we play for the room. If you win, we will immediately surrender it to you just as it stands; if, on the contrary, you lose, you shall bind yourself to depart and never molest us again."

Agonized at the ever-darkening mysteries that seemed to thicken around me, and despairing of being able to dissipate them by the mere exercise of my own will, I caught almost gladly at the chance thus presented to me. The idea of my loss or my gain scarce entered into my calculations. All I felt was an indefinite knowledge that I might, in the way proposed, regain in an instant, that quiet chamber and that peace of mind of which I had so strangely been deprived.

"I agree!" I cried eagerly; "I agree. Anything to rid myself of such unearthly company!"

The woman touched a small golden bell that stood near her on the table, and it had scarce ceased to tinkle when a negro dwarf entered with a silver tray on which were dice-boxes and dice. A shudder passed over me as I thought in this stunted African I could trace a resemblance to the ghoul-like black servant to whose attendance I had been accustomed.

"Now," said my neighbour, seizing one of the dice-boxes and giving me the other, "the highest wins. Shall I throw first?"

I nodded assent. She rattled the dice, and I felt an inexpressible load lifted from my heart as she threw fifteen.

"It is your turn," she said, with a mocking

smile; "but before you throw, I repeat the offer I made you before. Live with us. Be one of us. We will initiate you into our mysteries and enjoyments, — enjoyments of which you can form no idea unless you experience them. Come; it is not too late yet to change your mind. Be with us!"

My reply was a fierce oath, as I rattled the dice with spasmodic nervousness and flung them on the board. They rolled over and over again, and during that brief instant I felt a suspense, the intensity of which I have never known before or since. At last they lay before me. A shout of the same horrible, maddening laughter rang in my ears. I peered in vain at the dice, but my sight was so confused that I could not distinguish the amount of the cast. This lasted for a few moments. Then my sight grew clear, and I sank back almost lifeless with despair as I saw that I had thrown but *twelve*!

"Lost! lost!" screamed my neighbour, with a wild laugh. "Lost! lost!" shouted the deep voices of the masked men. "Leave us, coward!" they all cried; "you are not fit to be one of us. Remember your promise; leave us!"

Then it seemed as if some unseen power caught me by the shoulders and thrust me toward the door. In vain I resisted. In vain I screamed and shouted for help. In vain I implored them for pity. All the reply I had was those mocking peals of merriment, while, under the invisible influence, I staggered like a drunken man toward the door. As I reached the threshold the organ pealed out a wild triumphal strain. The power that impelled me concentrated itself into one vigorous impulse that sent me blindly staggering out into the echoing corridor, and as the door closed swiftly behind me, I caught one glimpse of the apartment I had left forever. A change passed like a shadow over it. The lamps died out, the siren women and masked men vanished, the flowers, the fruits, the bright silver and bizarre furniture faded swiftly, and I saw again, for the tenth of a second, my own old chamber restored. There was the acacia waving darkly; there was the table littered with books; there was the ghostly lithograph, the dearly beloved smoking-cap, the Canadian snow-shoes, the ancestral dagger. And there, at the piano, organ no longer, sat Blokeeta playing.

The next instant the door closed violently, and I was left standing in the corridor stunned and despairing.

As soon as I had partially recovered my comprehension I rushed madly to the door, with the dim idea of beating it in. My fingers touched a cold and solid wall. There was no door! I felt all along the corridor for many yards on both sides. There was not even a crevice to give me hope. I rushed downstairs shouting madly. No one answered. In the vestibule I met the negro; I seized him by the collar and demanded my room. The demon showed his white and awful teeth, which were filed into a saw-like shape, and extricating himself from my grasp with a sudden jerk, fled down the passage with a gibbering laugh. Nothing but echo answered to my despairing shrieks. The lonely garden resounded with my cries as I strode madly through the dark walls, and the tall funereal cypresses seemed to bury me beneath their heavy shadows. I met no one, — could find no one. I had to bear my sorrow and despair alone.

Since that awful hour I have never found my

room. Everywhere I look for it, yet never see it. Shall I ever find it?

*****

THE END